Rock 'n' Roll Confessions

Book I

Helena Danyluk

authorHOUSE®

AuthorHouse™
1663 Liberty Drive, Suite 200
Bloomington, IN 47403
www.authorhouse.com
Phone: 1-800-839-8640

First published by AuthorHouse 4/6/2009

ISBN: 978-1-4389-5050-1 (sc)

Printed in the United States of America
Bloomington, Indiana

This book is printed on acid-free paper.

Present

Rock 'N' Roll Confessions #1

She walks into the dark, smoky room, searching for the darkest, most mysterious stranger. Lust is burning like an insatiable hunger. Her red stilettos seem to scream more like the bass of a guitar than heels clicking on the hardwood floor. She can feel the black seam of her thigh-high stockings burning up the backs of her legs. She approaches the bar. The bartender wipes a glass clean with his somewhat dirty towel.

"What can I get ya?" he asks, eyeing her up and down, drinking her in like a tall cold one. He can feel his manhood pulsing in between his legs. But he knows he has nothing more to offer her than a martini that tastes like Skittles. He can see her hunger. She licks her lips and tugs gently at the edge of her lower lip with her teeth. She has the whitest teeth he has ever seen, he notes. And he can only imagine what that soft, sexy mouth can do. Nude lips, piercing green eyes, with a hint of witchery. *This one is up to no good,* he tells himself.

She answers, "Something sweet, but strong," in a raspy, seductive voice. Slowly she removes her leather jacket and hangs it on the back of the bar stool. The cool air whispers across her chest and makes her already perky tits stand erect.

He almost drops the martini. "There's one lucky bastard in here tonight," he thinks out loud.

"I'm sorry, what was that?" she asks, her voice luring him in.

"Sorry, nothing, just talkin' out loud. This one is on the house. You looking for someone?" He almost feels like he has to get away from her. His cock is throbbing so hard she can probably hear it.

"I found him. Thanks." She raises the drink in her hand, swings her jacket over her shoulder, and saunters over to the corner.

She found him all right. Always the dark one in the corner of the bar, strumming some melancholy song on that old guitar of his, his dark hair hanging over his eyes. His legs spread open, revealing a rip a tad too high in his jeans.

He feels her before he sees her. Only one woman can make his heart stop and his cock go before she even touched him. But it had been years. Before he even looked up, he knew it was her. Her heels were slicing into him just like those piercing eyes. He felt them burn through him, seeing his soul, his heart. How did she always find him when he needed her most? He played it cool and kept his head down.

She didn't say anything. She just pulled up a chair, slid into it, and crossed those long, damn sexy legs. He saw her red spikes, his favorite color, and followed the black stockings up until he met her stare dead on.

"Hey," was all he could muster without falling to the floor and spreading those legs that went on for miles and diving into the most delectable woman he had ever been with. And there were a lot of women. He had to remain composed. She looked so in control.

"Well, hello there. Miss me?" She gave a twisted smile. It was a smile that meant she came to play and play hard. Her eyes danced with mischief as she raised a perfectly shaped eyebrow.

"Always." She was killing him. How did she remain so unnerved? He should have told her no. Or even maybe. Now it's her game.

"I didn't come to play games with you," she whispered in his ear and then tugged gently at his lobe.

"I've missed you. That's all. And I thought it was time I come to find you." She remained composed on the outside, but inside her body burned. When she crossed her legs, she could feel the wetness slipping down. She trembled inside. She had to have him soon. She knew he was the only one who could fill the emptiness the hunger left, the ache that made her come for him again and again. And he wouldn't disappoint. She could tell he was up to the challenge, however calm he wanted her to believe he was. He placed his guitar back in the case.

"Don't stop on my account. I could listen to you play all night. But I'd rather you play me."

That was all it took. He lost all composure and grabbed her by the waist, pulling her chair over to his, forcing her to open her legs. In one quick movement, she had her legs around his waist and was sitting on his lap. His cock was standing at attention, rubbing through his jeans onto her panties. His mouth pressed down hard on hers. Rough passion—he wasn't going to take it easy on her. He wanted her to pay for leaving him for so long.

She welcomed the aggression. Succumbed to it. Reaching down in between them, she slid his member out of the constricting jeans, and he gasped. So much passion. Wild, reckless. How could he have forgotten how much she made him ache? Wild, no consequences. Shit, they were still in the bar!

She wanted him now, here. Panting as they ravaged each other, she had her hands tangled in his hair, pulling him closer, deeper.

"Now," she moaned.

"Now," she said in hushed tones.

His hand was in her silky panties; he pulled them to the side and slid in. He felt his mind, body, and heart melt into the slippery folds of her hot pussy. This, this is where he belonged—in her.

She screamed as he entered her. Right here in the middle of some second-rate bar, in the darkest corner, with the bartender watching with disbelieving eyes. This is where she belonged—with him.

Rock 'N' Roll Confessions #2

She bolted straight up, breathing heavy. Wow. *What a dream,* she thought to herself, only to realize he was sleeping peacefully beside her. Not a dream. Real. She often dreamt of seeing him again, but with so many road trips of his and business adventures of hers, it just couldn't happen. And yet, here she was, with him, with his seed still running down her legs. She wrapped the navy blue sheet around her naked body and got up to figure this out. This hadn't happened to her in years, not remembering how she ended up in bed with these men. Well, only one man. Him. Always him. *How,* she thought. How did she find him? Why did she find him? He had hurt her so many times. All those other woman … always leaving her in search for the next gig. Until, she finally left him, for good. Until now.

It's that blinding urge for passion—the urge, need, or crazy-ass head of hers! *What the hell am I going to do now?* she asked herself.

She searched for his cigarettes. Hopefully he still smoked. She hadn't in years but was now in desperate need of one. There they were, on the dresser beside her torn panties. Hmm. That kind of night, was it? She should realize or remember with the way her lips still ached and her inner thighs felt bruised. Oh, she needed to sit down. This was too much to take in. Grabbing an ashtray, she sat in the lazy boy chair in the corner that was covered with the rest of her clothing. Throwing them to the floor, she dropped down into the chair and hauled on her cig.

Watching him in his deep sleep, she thought, *Yeah, you always did get a good night's sleep after me.* They wore each other out, as usual. She tried to remember the night. She saw flashes of hot, sweaty erotic sex. No, not just sex—raw fucking. Raw, savage fucking. The bar.

Riding him on the wooden chair in the back of the bar—that's where it started. She remembered walking into that bar with the hopes of seeing him there. She remembered the small conversation they had, the sounds coming from his guitar. The look in his eyes when his eyes finally met hers. She had felt so confident, so sure of herself. She always was. Yet in the dark hours of the morning, sitting here, she doubted herself. She saw more flashes.

The parking lot.

They couldn't keep their hands off each other. His hands were wrapped up in her hair, tangled at the back of her neck, grabbing passionately, drinking her in. She could taste the blood on her lips from biting and kissing. Pulling her closer, he wanted to swallow her whole and fill her every opening with him. He missed her. She could feel his hunger; it was as deep as her own. He drove his hard, swollen member so hard against her. He wanted her to know his need for her. She couldn't breathe. Lust was blinding her—always blinding her. Her aching body was the only thing keeping her standing. She grabbed at the long strands of hair, winding them around her fingers until he pushed her on her back onto the hood of the 1967 black mustang a little rougher than expected.

"I need this. Now. I can't wait. I've waited too long. And it's mine. I'm taking it back!" he rasped out, mad lust in his voice.

He ran his hands down the length of her body, pushed up her skirt, and slid his hands teasingly onto her inner thighs.

"Now," he teased, "did you miss me?" He was in total control now.

She cried, "Yes. Yes, I missed you." Tears rolled down her cheeks and landed on the hood of his car. His teasing continued. First small licks on the inner thighs, then small kisses turning a little harder. He couldn't take it anymore, and she was shaking.

"Now, did you miss me?" he asked again.

"Yes." She mustered a whisper, the tears pouring out of her now. He made her crazy with yearning. It was a game they had played for years, but until now she hadn't realized how much she had missed him or needed him, for that matter.

"Louder. I can't hear you. I want everyone to hear you." He played her clit like the strings of his guitar, and he could see it glistening under the streetlights. He wanted in there. He tasted her slowly at first, until he just couldn't take it any longer himself, so he feasted, lapped up as much of her as he could. He could taste her cum. She was the most delectable woman he had ever been with. She tasted like candy that you just can't get enough of. Addictive. That's what she was, and she knew it.

"Yes, yes, YES! I need you now. I miss you so much!" she sobbed. She couldn't handle it any longer. And he took her, banging her on the hood of his car, grabbing frantically at each other. He licked the salty tears off her face. Those damn eyes, glowing in the dark with passion, fear, and something else. He came hard and fast. And then fell on top of her. "You're mine. Always were," he whispered with a hint of malevolence.

And now here she was, in his house. In his bedroom. Smoking his cigarettes. She took one last haul on the cig and grabbed her clothes.

He slept.

Rock 'N' Roll Confessions #3

She dressed quickly, leaving behind her torn panties as a reminder. Hell, she couldn't wear them again anyway. Quietly, she tiptoed around his house in the dark. She didn't want to wake him. She had to get out of here before he woke up. It was just too much.

Too wild, too reckless.

With her heels in her hand, she reached for the door and banged into a table. "Damn!" She covered her mouth and tried to stop the table from tipping over and spilling its content. Too late. She turned on the side lamp to try to clean up before she bolted, yet again. She didn't have time to start this all over again. She didn't want another relationship, especially this kind, the kind that left her head spinning. She bent over to pick up the papers that had fallen to the floor, wincing in pain. Oh, it was a good session all right. *I'll pay for this for the next few days*, she thought to herself.

She gathered the papers together, and then she saw it. The picture. Just a head shot.

Their heads were touching, and they had the biggest smiles. Oh my God, how could he still have this? She smiled with a short laugh to herself. She looked at the picture of the night they first met. Oh, had they changed. There was a lot of bad hair back then. But there she was, bad hair and all, with the biggest naïve smile.

It was 1992 the year she met him. He had just come home from LA, the place all rockers went to become rock stars, and where all the girls wished they could go, herself included. She sat and listened to his stories all night, from a distance. She was new to the scene and very young, not quite shy, but not worldly enough for him. He noticed her.

Introduced himself with the cheesiest line, and she fell for it.

She was sweetly seductive, yet he knew she didn't know it. Not yet, but when she got older … she was gonna be a heartbreaker. He wanted her in that little dress that showcased her long, lean legs. The dress was way too short, and he loved it. It was a mental picture he kept for the rest of his life.

They chatted for a bit, and he led her to a quiet room in the house.

"You're gorgeous, you know that?" he smoothed his way in. He sat beside her on the bed. *Maybe she did know,* he thought.

"Thanks." she smiled innocently enough, but there was something behind those eyes that wasn't so innocent. She reached up and touched his hair. "A little too much spray," she teased. She decided she needed to take control of this. She climbed onto his lap like she was riding him.

"That move could get you in trouble," he teased outwardly, but he knew there was some truth to his words.

"Really, what kind of trouble?" she teased right back, tilting her head slightly to the side.

She knew what she was doing, and before she gave him the chance to answer, she placed her soft lips over his.

Juicy, he thought. And so fucking soft. She kissed older than what she was. He knew she was young, so he wanted to tread carefully. But with lips like that, it was going to be very hard.

She felt him grow beneath her. She started to grind around on his lap, intensifying the moment. The kissing grew heavier. He flipped her over onto the bed, "I told you that move would get you into trouble!" He explored her body from head to toe, giving feather touches up her legs, her arms, sliding the straps of that little dress off her shoulders.

He pulled the dress all the way down, until it passed her feet. He tossed the dress to the side.

More feather touches up her legs.

She shivered. She was nervous now. Her heartbeat quickened. He was older, and she knew he'd wanted more. It wasn't like she was a virgin, but no high school boyfriend had touched her like this!

He slowed down. He could feel her tensing up.

"Are you okay?" he asked. "You don't have to worry, I won't hurt you. I just want to," he broke off his sentence and started kissing her again. Damn, she tasted so good. Sweet, like candy. He couldn't keep his hands off her.

"I'm fine, keep going." The room was spinning from the alcohol and the heat of the room. She started breathing heavy as he slid his fingers inside her. She moaned loudly.

He was kissing her belly, licking her hip bones, all the while spinning his fingers inside her.

Her head spun faster, and she felt something in her building, climbing. She felt like climbing the walls, but he held her there. He held her while he spun those fingers around and around, in and out. She wanted to scream. She probably did. She had never felt anything like this before.

He was whispering something; she had no idea of what he was saying at this point.

"Now, now, now," she squealed. And they both felt the gush of liquid that spilled out of her. He lay beside her.

"I want more. But I can wait. Have you ever had an orgasm before?" he asked.

"No," was the only word from her mouth. She couldn't move.

She stood up with the picture still in hand.

"What's that?" he asked before he realized she was about to leave him again.

.

Rock 'N' Roll Confessions #4

"Were you going to leave? Without saying a word?" his voice was slowly rising as he stood there naked. "Were you just gonna let me sleep as you walked out the door? What the fuck is your problem? Why do you do this?" Not giving her the chance to speak, he was almost yelling now. He slammed his fist against the wall beside her head. She didn't even blink.

She just stared at him. She had planned to leave without a word. But seeing that picture brought back so many memories.

He hung his head down in defeat. "I can't believe you're doing this again." He had lowered his voice now.

She raised her hand to touch his face. Tears. She felt tears. She had never known him to show his feelings.

"I'm sorry. I just …" He cut her off before she had the chance to finish.

"No. I'm sorry. I'm sorry I let you do this. I'm sorry you can't let anyone in. I thought the party girl would have grown up after all these years. It's not just sex anymore! I thought when you walked into that bar you were coming back. I thought you needed me!" He placed his hand on top of hers.

"I can't let you go. Not this time." His voice remained calm and quiet.

She reached up and took his face in both of her hands. "I was going to leave. I was. I thought it was just sex with us. And then I saw the picture. I can't believe you still have the picture." She searched his soulful eyes for something more. She needed more.

"Just sex? Is that all you ever wanted from me?" His voice was starting to grow louder.

"No, I …" Again, he didn't let her finish.

"Just sex, eh? I'll give you just sex!" He was mad with lust, seeing her at that door, about to walk out on him again. He couldn't even hear what she was saying anymore.

Her defenses were up now! How dare he? Who the hell did he think he was?

"Oh fuck you!" she yelled. "You don't own me! No one owns me! I own me! And if you let me finish my damn sentence, you would know that I'm not leaving again!" She yelled in his face, and he could see that fierceness growing in her eyes. Glowing green, they always got greener when she was mad.

She was about to let him have it, when he wrapped his hands around her wrists and pinned her up against the door and went in for a wild, fierce lip lock, when he stopped just in front of her lips. He could feel her breath on his mouth. They were both breathing heavily. She stared that bewitching stare. She was inviting the fight; she would always fight. He knew that. But he didn't want to fight anymore. Too many years of fighting, and where did it get them? More wild sex, which ended with her walking out the door and him not seeing her for a few months, sometimes years.

"I can't. I just can't do it again," he whispered. Then he gently kissed her. Softly, like the first time they met.

She allowed the anger to slip away and kissed him back. He lifted her legs up so she sat on the table, and she wrapped her legs around his waist. *Gentle*, he thought, *like that night in the picture.* She seemed so young, so vulnerable then. And he wanted to take care of her then. *So why hadn't I*, he asked himself.

He caressed her arms as she ran them up his bare chest tracing the tattoos with her fingers. Her head slightly down, just enough to let her hair fall over her face.

He let his hands fall to her hips, slightly squeezing her ass as he pulled himself in. He knew she was tender, bruised from the night before. And with the orange glow of morning rising up behind them, peaking through the window, he made love to her for the first time in all the years they'd known each other. He took her slowly, caressing every inch of her body with feather touches. She was so soft, like silk. Her hands glided over his body, and she kissed those soft kisses on his shoulders, his neck, his face and sucked gently on his lower lip. He slid in and out of her as slowly as he could. Savoring every movement, she leaned her head back, exposing her swan-like neck. And they came together, in more ways than one.

He lifted her up and carried her back to bed. She lay down beside him and slept in his arms.

They woke in the morning to the radio playing one of his ballads.

"Oh, this is my favorite song of yours. I loved this whole CD. Your best one yet," she proudly said to him. He was very talented.

"You should love it! Every song is about you!" he confessed to her, something he never thought he would do.

The Past

Rock 'N' Roll Confessions #5

As he lay in bed, he thought back to the year he recorded that album.

He bent over, straw in hand, and snorted yet another line. Some hot chick was hanging off his back waiting for her turn. He shrugged her off and turned to walk away.

"Where ya goin', baby?" she slurred. This chick was so fucking strung out she didn't know what guy she was here with. Damn groupies. The attention was great, and it was too easy to get laid. But sometimes it was too much. He'd been partying for days now, celebrating the record deal he'd just signed. Finally all his hard work had paid off.

"Hey man, line 'em up!" His band member grabbed him around the neck and pulled him in, rubbing his head with his knuckles.

He shook his head free. "I just went. You go without me." He was hot. There were a lot of people in here. And everyone kept touching him, grabbing him; girls were kissing him all over the place. One girl even grabbed his balls and demanded he fuck her tonight.

He was starting to panic; he felt his eyes bulging out of his head. His heart was racing; he started to sweat. He wiped at his nose. It was beginning to get raw.

He tried to find the door, the balcony, anywhere outside. He needed air. He finally made it outside. He started walking down the street when he spotted a girl getting into her car. He quickened his pace. It couldn't be her. She was in Paris or some shit.

"HEY!" He found himself running toward the girl and her car, yelling. She stopped and turned around. Not her.

He stopped dead in the street. He was so sure it was going to be her. He wanted to see her, share the good news. She always knew he'd get signed.

"Sorry, wrong person." The cool air snapped him out of it for a few minutes. He stood still, trying to adjust his eyes.

"Hey man, where you goin'? The party's just getting good in there. There are a couple of girls dancin' naked together on the table! Get your ass in here!" His buddy was beaming from ear to ear.

" Nowhere. I'm coming. Where are these girls?" He wanted to seem interested in what his friend was talking about, but he'd had enough for the night.

"Just think, now that we're signed, this is what it's gonna be like! Twenty-four seven party and chicks, man!"

"Yeah, great." He was still too fucking high when he walked back in. There he spotted the crowd of people around the two girls. As he looked around, it seemed like everyone was getting naked! The girls his friend had been talking about were now making out with each other.

"FUCK YEAH!" His buddy screamed and tore off his shirt as he dove into the heart of the scene. "I LOVE BEING FAMOUS!" Laughter roared through the crowd.

Someone yelled back, "We're not famous yet, but we will be soon!" The crowd cheered and roared.

He couldn't help but get caught up in the excitement. A girl came up behind him and asked, "Wanna get outta here?"

He turned and kissed her hard on the mouth.

"You wanna be with a rock star?" his hoarse voice hushed out. He led the girl outside and into a cab.

He grabbed the girl's head and pushed it down into his lap. She giggled and pulled out his member and slid it right into her mouth. He groaned as he rested his head on the back of the cab's seat, enjoying the warm, moist in-and-out sensation. He opened his eyes to see why the cab driver hadn't moved yet. Just as he was about to yell at the guy, he looked over to where the cab driver stared.

Only to see her standing on the sidewalk all dressed in black. She looked so hot. No wonder the cabbie couldn't drive away. She had that effect on men. But he could see the hurt in her eyes.

She held up a bottle of champagne as if to cheer him, and with a malicious smile and a tilt of the head, she smashed it down on the sidewalk and stormed away. He watched as she walked away, swinging that ass. She stuck her middle finger in the air.

He was too fucking high to think.

"Fuck. FUUUUUUCKKKK!" he yelled.

"GO. JUST GO!" He yelled to the cabbie.

The girl looked up at him. "What's up. baby? Doesn't it feel good?" Her eyes were glazed over, her pupils the size of quarters.

"Fine. Everything is just fucking great." He pushed his hair back from his sweaty brow and closed his eyes. No wonder she always left him.

Rock 'N' Roll Confessions #6

As she faded back into the sweet seduction of sleep, she fell into the past.

She'd been living in Paris for two years now; her lover lay in her bed. Lazy bastard. She hated when he stayed the night. She wished he would just fuck her and go home. She wasn't the romantic, relationship kind of girl. He was good in bed, though, whispering terms of endearment in her ear as he pleasured her body—her entire body. She'd learned a few new tricks from him, all right. But hell, he could've been reciting his grocery list for all she knew. Two years, and she still didn't know the language.

She was growing tired of this city and ached for home.

When she arrived here, she was eager to meet new people, learn new culture and tradition. She needed the change. She wanted to meet new men, seduce them, and leave them. It was something she knew how to do well.

And there had been a lot of French men eager to fall for her. It was almost too easy. She missed the fight, the chase. She missed him. She was starting to feel that need for him again. It had been two years since she had last seen him. She wondered what he was up to, wondered if he'd given up on his music or had finally been signed. She hoped he was still pursuing it. He was extremely talented.

As she downed the remnants of last night's wine from its sleek goblet, she felt that urge, that emptiness, the hunger left that only he could fill. Her French lovers were fantastique, but no one touched her the way he did. No one had compared to that first night she met him. No one could feed that hunger the way he did.

She shoved her lover's leg with her well-pedicured foot.

"Get up, mon cher." She pushed at him again. Now she would lose her patience.

"Get up! I'm leaving. You have to go!" Her voice was stern.

He rolled over still half asleep, rambling in half French, half English, "Where are you going, mon cher?' He reached up to pull her back into the tussled sheets.

"Come back to bed. I'm cold. I need you to warm me up." He sulked, something he did that used to turn her on. Something she used to fall for.

"Oh, stop sulking! I hate it when you do that!" She turned away from him, lit a cigarette, and exhaled.

"I'm going home. To Canada. You have to get out of my bed. I'm leaving tonight," she stated before realizing that was exactly what she wanted to do. The sooner, the better.

"You're leaving me? Why? I thought we were so good together. Look, here." He reached in the pocket of his designer jeans and pulled out a petite ring box.

"I wanted to wait to give this to you, but ..." He crawled out of bed and went down on one knee.

"Oh no you don't! I told you not to fall for me. This was just sex. Lots of great sex and no ties!" He would be the third Frenchman to propose to her.

He was passionately angry with her. "Why don't you let me in? Why don't you let anyone in? I love you. I want to marry you." Oh, she had heard this before. What was wrong with having a good time? Enjoying each other. Partying together. Why did they all have to get serious?

She'd have to be gentle with this one. He was so passionate. So emotional. The Europeans were, more so than the rough and tough Canadian boys. The thought made her long for home that much more.

She pulled him up and sat on the bed, and he sat beside her, hurt, scorned.

She healed him the only way she knew how. She got down on her knees, running her hands up his legs, kissing his inner thighs, rubbing his manhood as she explained she just had to go home. Her parents needed her there. A lie, only she knew. She whispered she'd miss him and never forget him. She told him, he'd always hold a special place in her heart. She seduced him into his goodbye, his "au revoir." And she thoroughly enjoyed him one last time. Her last French lover.

She would remember the way his mouth tasted after he had pleasured her. She would remember the slow slide of his thickness, the rough way he took her up against the door as she clung to the doorframe to keep from going through the glass door. She would remember his hands on her body. And she would remember the door slamming as he walked out, smashing the glass, as she had just smashed his heart. And she would remember the emptiness he couldn't fill. And that's why she was going home.

To find him. To feed that hunger.

She arrived at the airport exhausted and excited. Her best friend was meeting her there. And she had very exciting news for her. It was a surprise. Her friend told her it was worth the wait and she'd be very excited. She knew it must be about him. She almost expected him to be there to pick her up. But as she rolled her bag into the pick-up area, she realized it was just her best friend. He hadn't come. Ecstatic to see her best friend, she dropped everything and ran to hug her.

"I want details! About EVERYTHING!" Her friend threw her arms around her, and they hugged like sisters.

"I missed you too!" she laughed.

"So what's the big news? I can't wait any longer; I thought about it the whole flight. Now tell me, or I won't give you any juicy details. Or the very expensive gift I bought for you." She giggled, teasing her friend.

"Well, thanks, I'm doing great. Thanks for asking!" she said sarcastically.

She tilted her head. "We'll get to all that later! Now tell me!" she demanded as they grabbed her bags and headed for the car.

"Okay, are you ready? You couldn't have come home at a better time. He got signed! And there's a huge signing party for the band tomorrow night!"

"AHHHHH." They both screamed and jumped up and down.

"Does he know I'm back?"

"No. I thought we could surprise him tomorrow at the party. For sure, you're going, right?" she asked, even though she knew the only reason her friend had come back was for him. She missed him and needed him again.

And he needed her. He had to straighten out again. And she knew this was the only girl who could do it.

"Of course I'm going! We're going! Oh, I knew he would get signed! How does he look? Does he talk about me still? He must be so excited! I can't wait to see him! Wait till you see the sexy little black outfit I just bought in Paris. He's gonna cum on the spot when he sees me!"

The next night, she was running late and told her friend she'd meet up with her at the party. Jet lag. She had slept all day and most of the night. She was now frantically getting ready. She didn't want to be too late.

She jumped in the cab with a bottle of champagne to celebrate with him.

As she pulled up, she saw him walking toward another cab. She yelled his name, but the music was so loud, even out here on the sidewalk.

She sauntered over to the cab he was getting into—with another girl. She stopped dead as she watched him pull the girl's head down to give him head. She just watched and thought, *You fucking prick. You haven't changed a bit!* She made eye contact with him. She saw the glazed look in his eyes, then the delayed shock of seeing her. There was a flash of excitement for her before he realized what he was doing in the cab with that other girl and what she was doing to him. She held up the champagne bottle in a toast and then smashed in on the ground and walked away. Again.

Rock 'N' Roll Confessions #7

He showed up at her door two days later. And he looked like shit. She didn't want to let him in, but her friend had explained the recent drug use, and the fact that he didn't know she was home. She had been gone to Paris for two years.

Fuck, fine, whatever. She let him in.

"You look like shit," she matter-of-factly stated as she opened the door to let him in. She turned to walk back into the apartment.

"You look fucking hot." He tried to smooth his way back in. But he did think she looked hot.

Her heart was pounding. She was still angry. No, she was furious. She'd had mental pictures of that slut sucking him off for the last two days. But she wouldn't let him know that she cared so much.

"I know. Want something to drink?" She reached into the fridge, bending so her g-string would peak out the top of her jeans. She knew he was checking her ass out.

"Just water. If you got it." He was mildly amused. He could see the anger in her, even though she was doing her best to hide it. Anyone else would never catch on. But he knew her inside out.

She threw a water bottle at him hard enough that he almost dropped it. Instead, it made a "thug" noise against his chest.

She sat on the other couch, not beside him. *Okay*, he thought, *she isn't going to make this easy.*

"Baby, if I knew you were coming home, I would never have gone home with that other girl." He was trying to sweet talk her, even though he knew he really didn't do anything wrong.

"Oh, I don't care. I don't own you. You can do what you want. Remember? No strings." She twisted that evil smile of hers on him. She was pissed right off. He could see right through her.

"You don't have to be mad. Really, she didn't mean anything. Just wanted to get my rocks off. Celebrate a bit. You know," he tried to explain, make it seem like nothing—which it was. What she didn't see was as soon as they rounded the corner, he told the girl to go back to the party. After seeing her, he just wanted to be alone. Well, actually, he wanted to be with her. But he knew better than to go to her that night. So instead, he went home and wrote six songs for his new album, all of them about her.

"You don't owe me anything. Actually, I'll be leaving for Paris soon. I'm engaged. I just came home to get the rest of my shit and then head back over. Thought I would pop by to congratulate you before I left." When she spoke, she lacked emotion.

He knew she was lying, but her words still infuriated him.

"Fuck you!" he plainly said.

"No, FUCK YOU! You dirty prick!" She broke her restraint. "I come home to see you, and what do I see? Some bitch sucking your dick! I knew I should've stayed away from you! I was right to leave. And right to leave again. I fucking hate you!" She was yelling, and the tears were streaming down her face. Her eyes glowed. She paced the room as she yelled.

"So I was getting my dick sucked? Big fucking deal! What else was I supposed to do while you were over in Paris with Pierre, or Francois or PETE! Don't tell me you didn't suck them off! Or that they didn't French kiss your pussy! You were probably fucking everything you could find over there! You and your insatiable hunger for sex! Which, by the way, I think is bullshit!" He stood up and yelled right in her face.

She slapped him right across the face. And then she slapped the other cheek.

"You. Get out of my house. Don't come back. Forget you know me. Forget my name." She spoke softly. He had never hurt her with words like that before. She walked toward the window and kept her back turned to him.

She wasn't fighting. Oh shit. She always fought back. He thought she would fight back and then they would have wild, passionate sex all night and they'd be good. But he knew as the words left his mouth, he had pushed her too far. He regretted those words as soon as they left his lips. He was so jealous of her life in Paris. He didn't want anyone touching her, especially some fucking French guy.

"Oh, and his name is Eric," she said without turning around.

He ran at her, spun her around, and pinned her up against the wall.

"Let me go, you ass! Don't you dare touch me!" She was yelling at him, and he saw the tear-stained cheeks. He knew he hurt her this time.

"Fuck Eric! You won't marry him anyway! You always leave. You left him, and that's why you're back! You left him the way you leave everyone. The way you left me." He lunged in for her mouth.

She bit him and drew blood.

He ripped her tank top wide open, exposing her perky tits. She tore at his shirt, clawed him with her blood-red nails, leaving wicked welts on him.

"I don't want you," she sneered. Vicious eyes scorched him

"Yes you do, and it doesn't matter. I want you." He sucked her tits hard, pulling them into his mouth as far as he could.

She tangled her hands in his long hair, no spray, and pushed his head into her chest. She wanted to make him choke on her tits.

He pulled at his torn jeans with one hand and hers with the other. He ripped her g-string off with his teeth as he used his feet to pull at the legs of his pants. He rammed his fingers inside her tight pussy. She squealed. He followed up with his tongue. He was on his knees now, sucking the life out of her lips. Her juices flowed over his tongue, his face. She was moaning now, pushing his head further in. She kicked him over with her foot.

"You want to get your cock sucked? I'll suck it. I'll suck it so hard that every time you have it sucked you'll still feel me!" She turned into that wild, sadistic lover that only she could be. She was trying to fill that hunger. He could see it in her eyes.

She deep throated the entire thing and then slowly circled her tongue around and around as she moved back up towards the tip, flicking quickly over the tiny slit in the head. Her lips were creating a fast suction on the head, and he thought he would explode. She flicked that wild tongue down the side of his shaft as she jerked it roughly with her one hand; she fondled his testicles until she took them in whole in her warm, moist mouth. She moved her fingers quickly in between his ass and balls and slowly circled the small, tender area. He shook. He had never felt anything so fucking amazing in his life. She swiveled around so he could suck her off at the same time. He welcomed the distraction. He was going to burst, explode in her mouth, on her face. She swung around again and rode his cock ferociously, up and down, circling her hips, fast, short, slow, long strides up and down. He screamed and trembled.

"Don't you dare cum yet. I'm not finished." The look in her eyes was devilish. He teased her clit to that glistening point when she was about to cum.

They climaxed together. She fell on top of him, and they slept on her living room floor in front of the window. He was sure her neighbors saw the whole thing.

Rock 'N' Roll Confessions #8

Hours later they woke. He told her all about his recording contract and how he was leaving for New York in the next few days.

"You should come with me. We can hang out in the streets of Manhattan together. Party like rock stars … just like we used to talk about," he said with a laugh. He was trying to convince her.

She played along for the conversation. "Well, why don't I meet you there? I have some business to attend to for work and home. I mean, I just got back, so I'm gonna need a few more days to get everything settled. But yeah, sounds good." She got up and slid back into her jeans. She had to get another top out of her room; he'd destroyed that one. She lost more clothing having sex with this guy. "Geez," she said out loud.

"Geez Louise!" he hollered back from the living room. He sounded like he was in such a good mood.

She didn't know if she could do this—go to New York with him. She had come back to be with him, but here. Not in New York. Should she give it a shot? Should she go to New York, play "the rock star couple"? She was starting to second-guess herself, when she realized the ache was gone. She hadn't even noticed until now. She was completely satisfied.

"You know what? I think I can get my stuff done in a few days. I'll come with you instead!" she shouted out to the living room as she pulled her favorite red tank top over her head.

He snuck up behind her and threw her on the bed, then jumped on top of her.

"Hmm, red, my favorite color, baby!" He nestled down into her shirt. She couldn't help but laugh. She realized she was happy. She was happy with him, like that first year.

"I'm so happy that you're coming. It wouldn't be the same without you."

"Me too. Now get off me, so I can get my shit done. Or else I won't be going with you." She rolled out of bed laughing. He tried to pull her back down. She squealed and ran out of the room.

Days later they were on the plane to New York, bags packed and heading off to their new adventure together.

He was totally stoked, as were the rest of the band, girlfriends included. The party began on the plane and didn't stop when they reached their destination.

The recording company had limos waiting for them. They all ran—well, some jumped and skipped—to the limos.

"Fuckin' eh, man!" The drummer yelled with his hands in the air, rocker style.

Champagne bottles popped, and they cruised into downtown New York, hanging out the windows, half loaded, singing "We Will Rock You!"

She was so happy she hadn't missed this. This was one of the biggest moments of his life, and she was right there with him.

He turned and kissed her as they drove past Times Square standing up, half hanging out of the sunroof.

Rock 'N' Roll Confessions #9

She walked up the ice-covered stairs to the large cement and glass building. Her six-inch heels were digging into the ice for traction. She hugged her long, black coat close to her body to keep her warm. New York was so bloody cold! *And everyone complains about Canadian winters,* she thought to herself. She headed into the recoding studio. He was still working on the album, and she thought she would surprise him. Only two of the girlfriends remained—herself and the drummer's girl.

Although she herself was not a girlfriend.

She was just a friend with all the benefits. She refused to cast herself as the girlfriend of a band member. She was her own agent. It worked better without the label. There was less stress. Lately, they hadn't been seeing each other too much anyway. She clubbed alone, and he worked on the album. That's probably why the other girls had left. They had gone back home to live their own lives. She was lucky enough that her work allowed her to work from anywhere in the world, or she may have left as well.

New York boasted many opportunities to meet new people, something she loved. She chalked it up to research. So she kept herself busy while he did his thing. She had to admit it was getting a bit boring for her anyway.

The first few months were filled with parties and nightclubs and meeting all sorts of executives from the business. Other bands that were already on tour came to meet them and hang out. The parties got out of control at times. There were so many girls coming around the band all the time that she wondered if she should even bother hanging around. Really, this was the life a rock star, and you either accepted it or walked away.

She opened the door to the studio, rubbing her hands together to warm them up. Even in her leather gloves, her fingers still tingled. The guys were just finishing up, sitting around on the couches, conceitedly praising themselves.

"Well, hello, hello boys," her raspy voice sang as she sauntered in. Swaying dramatically, she stopped in front of him. "Can I get your autograph … Mister?" She over-dramatized the question and then leaned in to kiss him on the cheek.

"What will you do for me?" He played along and pulled her on top of his lap. She couldn't help but laugh as he tickled her sides.

"How'd it go, guys? All done, yet?" she asked, hopeful.

All the guys threw in their two cents, talking at the same time.

"That good, eh?" she whispered in his ear.

"One more session and it should be finished," he told her.

The guys started to pack up their stuff, talking of food. Seems everyone was starving.

"Don't they feed you animals?" she asked and laughed.

"We're gonna go grab some food. You two coming?"

She was about to jump right up and run to the nearest restaurant. She had just realized she hadn't eaten since this morning, like twelve hours ago, when he piped up, "No, man, I'm tired. You go ahead. Think we'll just head home."

"I'm starving, aren't you?" she spoke quietly in his ear.

"Yeah, I'm starving, but I got all the food I need right here." He slid his hand in between her legs.

"Oh, really, Mister Rock Star ..." she said cheekily.

With everyone now gone, she seemed to forget her hunger—the real hunger for food—only to replace it with the hunger she felt for him.

"I missed you, baby." He held her close, kissing her neck, smelling her hair. "Sorry I haven't spent much time with you lately. Have you been a good girl?" he teased.

"Hmm. I've missed you too. And of course, I'm always good!" She exaggerated the word always. "But I have been lonely. When will you guys be done?"

"Like I said, one more session should do it. The only thing is, once they release the record, we'll be going on tour."

She stood back from him. "So that's what I walked in on tonight. A meeting of sorts. So, you go on tour soon, and?" She waited; she knew there was more to this story.

"Well, it's not me. I just want to say that first off. It's not me at all. But the guys …" she didn't let him finish.

"The guys think it's best that no girls come on the tour," she finished the sentence for him. "It's all good, babe. I think I'm done anyway." She felt mixed feelings. She didn't really want to go with him. She'd been thinking of a way to tell him for the last few days. But she was a little pissed that he brought it up so easily.

"What do you mean, you're done anyway? What the hell kind of answer is that?" He was starting to feel his anger and tension rise.

"No. Not like that. You know me; I hate being in one spot too long. And you're always so busy. And on tour, it's just going to get worse. Baby, we're good right now. Why ruin it? I'll meet you for sex-capades in different cities?" she ended with a sly question.

"You don't want to come?"

"Not really. Nothing personal, I just …" She didn't know how to finish. They weren't technically a couple. They never were. Yet lately that's how it was starting to feel. She wanted to change it before it would change for good, in a bad way.

She still had her arms around his neck, and his hands were around her waist.

"Wanna dance with me?" he asked.

"Sure." She lowered her eyes seductively.

"Our first slow dance and no music?" she stated.

"Oh wait," he went over to the switchboard thingy and magically made music come on. His music. It was a ballad she had never heard before, but it quickly became her favorite.

"Our first, but not our last dance, and now with music."

"I like it, I like it." She was talking about the song.

"Me too. Actually love it." He wasn't talking about the song.

They swayed slowly side to side, her hands around his neck, playing with his hair. She secretly wished he'd never cut it. He let his hands fall to her bum, seductively pulling her in so his growing member rubbed against her hips.

His hands ran the length of her body. As his hands touched the edges of her sweater dress, he pushed the sweater up and over her head and tossed it on the floor, leaving her in those wicked black thigh-highs with the line up the back, high heel boots, panties, and a lacy bra. She unbuttoned his shirt and slid her hands in. Skin on skin. Warm. They kissed as they danced, slow and sweet, exploring each other's bodies.

He picked her up and carried her over to the grand piano and sat her on top of it. He gave her feather touches up her legs, her belly, and her arms. Her legs spread open, inviting him in. He laid her on her back and slithered his way on top of her, kissing every inch of her on the way. On the way back down, he removed her bra, then her panties, and tossed them to the side with the rest of her clothes.

He'd been cautious this far, and now he couldn't handle it any longer. He kicked his shoes off, tore at his own clothes, and pulled her back up. He picked her up, her legs wrapped around his waist, and he thrust himself inside her over and over again. Sweaty and hot, they couldn't get enough. They moved over to the couch they had been sitting on earlier. She got on her knees and he took her from behind. Her head lifted as she peered over her shoulder to watch the expressions on his face.

"Harder!" she cried. "Deeper." She wanted to take all of him in. She wanted them to feel so close; they could be the same person.

He pulled at her long hair, forcing her head back and himself deeper. "Now, now, now," she moaned, louder with each call. He pushed himself in as far as he could go and came.

Rock 'N' Roll Confessions #10

She didn't see him as much as she thought she would. Phones calls became far and few between. But she was now heading backstage of the concert, where she'd wait for him until after the show. She watched from the sidelines, thoroughly enjoying the energy he put out while performing. He was covered in sweat. His hair hung wet and stuck to his face as he moved around the stage. He looked like he was having sex with his bass guitar, fingering the strings quickly with one hand and seductively caressing the arm of the bass with his other hand. She got wet just watching him, hoping he'd save enough energy to play her the same way later that night. She stood there smiling, without reason, just at the sight of him. She hadn't realized she'd missed him this much.

He shifted his gaze to where she was standing, and his face lit up.

She came, he thought. So many times before they had made plans, only to have them fall through. And yet here she was, standing on the side of the stage looking sexier than ever. He quickly noted something was different about her. He couldn't place it in the few seconds he took to steal a selfish glance at her, but he did see it. There was something else there behind those jade colored eyes and that sexy smile.

Maybe it was the fact that she wasn't some groupie, throwing her sex at him. Since being on tour, he'd had more pussy thrown at him; all the guys had. But it was almost too much. And most of the time he couldn't be bothered. These young ones were a little psycho for him—falling in love, calling the hotel room all hours of the night, stalkin' them out and shit. It was crazy shit that he just didn't have the time or the patience for. He was no angel on this fucked-up ride to stardom, but he was no idiot either.

He was getting hard, just thinking of her. He stole another glance, which confirmed the greeting in his tight pants. Thankfully, his guitar covered the secret war he was having with his dick right now.

Last encore done. He ran to her, picked her up, and swung her around.

"Eww. You're soaked in sweat!" she laughed. Yet it didn't stop her from holding on to him as tight as she could.

"How's this?" he shook his head, and the sweat sprayed like a wet dog all over her.

"You're so gross!" She tousled his hair with her hand.

"But I like it! That was a fabulous show! Lots of panties on that stage … should I throw you mine too?" she teased.

"Oh, no. You don't have to throw me your panties. I'm comin' to get 'em myself!" He reached for her ass, and she ran back to the dressing room. He followed howling like a dog.

The dressing room had a shower, so he striped off and turned on the water.

"I can't wait to touch you. Wanna join me?" he asked, hopeful. He wanted to touch her all over, she looked so damn good. She smelled good. He was sure she'd taste just as good.

"But my hair …" she said with a giggle as she slowly unbuttoned her tight pants and wiggled out of them dramatically. She wanted to dive on top of him sweat and all. She didn't care. It'd been months since she'd seen him last.

He tore at her clothes, kissed her passionately, and ran his hands up her back, slightly bending his knees. He wasn't sure if the show had made him weak or just the fact that she was standing in front of him. Naked. And he could have her anytime for the next three days.

He held her hand and led her into the shower. Hot water poured over their bodies as they kissed and touched everywhere they possibly could.

"So much for my hair!" she whispered. The feelings were so intense she thought she would explode if he didn't enter her now. Their hands were groping wildly, and his fingers wandered into every crevice of her body. He held her head with both hands, tangled in her hair, kissing her tender mouth. Open kisses with waterfalls of shower water ran between them. She held onto him tight. She didn't want to let him go. His body fit with hers like the piece of a puzzle. He pushed the hair back from her face and ran his lips and tongue up the side of her cheek. He flicked his head to get his soaking wet hair out of the way.

"Too much, hair. I should've put it up," she said.

"No, I like it," he hushed back.

She ran her tongue down his neck onto his chest and kissed every tattoo he had. Lowering herself to her knees, she took him into her mouth. Water pouring over her head, she opened her mouth to let the hot water in, and took him again. He let out a moan.

"Damn, baby. That feels fuckin' amazing!"

She held all seven inches in her mouth, slowly taking him in and out. She let the water spill from her mouth down her chin to land on the shower stall floor. He pulled her up to meet him face to face and kissed her.

"I missed you," he whispered.

He lifted her one leg and entered her. Slowly, he lifted himself into her. The hot water pushing inside her created friction. He leaned her up against the shower stall, holding her one arm above her head and his other hand holding onto her ass as his guide.

They couldn't stop kissing; she held his face to hers. They stared in each other's eyes, neither one wanting to look away. The moment intensified. She began to shake; he knew it was time. So he thrust harder, speeding up to satisfy her, and he reached around with his hand and played her clit like the strings of his bass, just the way she liked. Her moans quickly became lustful cries. Once he knew she couldn't handle it any longer, when he knew she was satisfied, he let himself go and felt the sticky rush of them spill out over his groin and run down his leg. The water, now cool, was washing it away.

Rock 'N' Roll Confessions #11

After the wild sex reunion, they went to an after-hours party for the band members, backstage pass holders, and hopeful groupies held in a very posh hotel penthouse suite.

The music was loud when they walked in. She walked through the room, initially holding his hand while he introduced her to all the new faces. Drink in hand, she mingled with new and old faces. She had a hard time wrapping their success around her mind. Not that they didn't deserve it. It was just that these were the same guys she had known for years and thought nothing more of them than just friends.

She couldn't help but notice the number of girls hanging off the guys, particularly the one that hadn't left his side since she got there. *Part of the package,* she thought to herself.

Some *GQ* Romeo type had been eyeing her all night and was now on his way over to talk to her. She glanced over to the bar and noticed he was chatting it up with a beautiful girl. *Part of the package,* she told herself again, although, this was getting to be a bit much to handle. She never thought of herself as the jealous type, although with him, she could very easily be. That's why she left labels such as "girlfriend" out of the equation. Romeo touched her arm.

"Hello, gorgeous. What are you doing standing alone?" He asked.

She rolled her eyes before turning to him and smiled that ferocious smile that could tear a man in two.

"Oh, I'm never alone. Are you enjoying yourself?" She turned on her professional personality that allowed her to talk to even the most obnoxious people. She was just standing there alone, taking in the party that now seemed to be stepping up a notch.

"I've been enjoying the view all night," he stated as he looked her up and down.

Could this guy be any cheesier? she thought to herself.

"This is my suite. I host parties here all the time for the bands coming through town. Best parties you'll ever attend," he boasted.

"Well, it seems everyone appreciates them." She didn't know how long she could talk to this guy. He was so obnoxious. But she didn't see a way out yet. And if the other one would take his eyes of that bitch, he might be able to come and save her. Hadn't she come here to spend all three days with him? Why was he on the other side of the room, and she was stuck here with the Hugh Hefner wannabe?

Romeo was babbling on about something, and she could feel herself nod in agreement even without hearing a word he said. She could feel the blood rising to her face as she stared across the room at him.

"Princess, you need something more than that martini. Come with me." He tugged at her hand.

"Oh, really I shouldn't, my friend is just over there. I should get back to him." She tried to step back.

"Which one? The one who's been talking to the other girl all night? Nice friend. If you were my friend, I wouldn't leave your side. I'd be afraid someone like me might sweep you off your feet. Which, by the way, I am trying to do, but you haven't heard a word I've said."

"Oh, I'm really sorry. I don't mean to be rude. I had a long flight today, and I'm starting to get tired. I was just thinking of heading out." She was tired—tired from the trip and tired of watching him mingle. She could start to feel the effects of all the martinis creep up on her.

Romeo put his arm around her waist. "I have just what you need. And you can bring your friend with you, if it makes you more comfortable." He leaned in to whisper in her ear. She tried to shy away from him without making it too noticeable.

At the same moment, he looked around the room to find her. He knew she would be pissed about the girl he'd been talking to all night. And it's not like he didn't try to get away from her. She just kept hanging on using the excuse of, "Just one more question." This girl was really trying to boost his ego, and he appreciated it, but he appreciated Her even more.

Where is she? He thought to himself as he scoped the room.

Then he spotted her standing next to host of the party—the last place he wanted her to be. This guy was filthy rich and took what he wanted, when he wanted. The guy was a good-looking, young, rich prick as far as he was concerned. He was living off Daddy's money, and he didn't want his filthy hands on her at all.

He excused himself, and the girl followed. He couldn't help but push his way through the crowd of people as he kept his eyes on her. That fucking prick had his arm around her shoulder. Why was she letting him touch her? What the hell was wrong with her?

"Hey, what's up?" he tried to cool himself down. He was the jealous type. Not that he had room to be, but she was his. She always had been, always would be, even if, she didn't know it yet.

"Hello, my friend. Great show tonight." Romeo held out his hand to him.

"Thanks. I see you've met my girl." He slid in beside her to claim his stake.

"Yes. She's beautiful; very sexy. Actually …" he didn't get to finish when she jumped in.

"I am standing right here, you know? I can hear you both elegantly battle out your male egos," she said sarcastically.

"Well, I was just inviting her, you as well, to come to my private room. It's much more comfortable." Romeo asked him instead of her, she noticed. *This is some sort of male ego thing,* she thought to herself. Well, let them. She was too tired and drunk to care at this point.

"Yeah, *we'll* come." Against his better judgment, he agreed to party in the private suite. You didn't say no to the host of this party. He had heard that from quite a few people. Or you didn't get another after-hours party thrown for your band.

"Great, my mistress will join us as well." He pulled the girl from the bar by the hand and led the way.

They gave each other a questioning glance.

Rock 'N' Roll Confessions #12

"Are you sure we should be going with this guy? He seems kinda out of it," she discussed in hushed tones with him.

"I can't say no. Do you know who this guy is?" He held her closer as they walked through the floor-to-ceiling mahogany doors.

"It'll be fine. Just stay close to me. Why were you talking to him anyway?" he asked, and she could hear the jealousy in his question.

"Well, why were you talking to his 'mistress' all night?" she asked back, and he noted the jealousy in her voice.

"I didn't know who she was, and we'll talk about this later. When we're alone."

With fake smiles, they entered the room. *Private all right,* she thought. This room was like a palace—a palace that was spinning. She suddenly felt the room spin. She was way too drunk for this.

"Sit down, make yourselves comfortable. What are you drinking?" their host asked.

"Oh, I don't need anymore, thanks. I think I've had too much already." She couldn't drink anymore, she thought. The room was starting to spin.

"Anything's fine," he said.

"Well, help yourself. It'll sober you up. Keep you going." He pointed to the mound of cocaine in the middle of the table and leaned in to snort a line himself. His mistress didn't say much, just joined him in a line.

Might as well, she thought after he did one too.

They laughed and talked for hours, it seemed. There were now relaxed. They were having a great time with this odd couple. They did line after line. The huge white mound never seemed to disappear. It must've been pure; she had never felt a high like this before. And somehow, she noticed, there was always a drink in front of her.

The music was on, some sort of slow, seducing music. Oh, she was so fucking high. They all were. Music. Line. Talk. Drink. It felt like a movie set, not real life, which always seemed to happen when toying with this drug.

The mistress squeezed in between them and took her hand.

"You have beautiful hands." *This is something only someone on heavy drugs would notice,* she thought to herself.

As she admired her hand, she traced the blue-red veins on the top of her hand and turned it over to look at her wrist. *What is this chick doing?* she thought to herself, but her light traces felt nice, so she didn't say anything.

"You have the softest skin," Mistress noted.

"Doesn't she?" she asked him as she turned back to look at him. She was practically on his lap.

"Yeah, she's super soft," he answered with a glint in his eye. He was enjoying this.

"No, really soft. Like freaky soft. You gotta touch her," she said to Romeo.

He reached over and touched her hand.

"Nice," was all he said, and he leaned back into his burgundy red leather chair to enjoy the view.

"Is she that soft everywhere?" the mistress teased him.

"Find out for yourself," he teased back.

Maybe it was the drugs or the alcohol. Or maybe it was the seductive seclusion of their night in this time warp of a room. But she really didn't mind the mistress touching her. She watched her hand trace up her arm and felt a tingling in her tummy. She looked over at the guys to watch for a reaction as she shifted her body toward the mistress, opening her legs just a bit. She could almost feel the rise in both of them as they shifted in their seats to accommodate their growing bulges.

She liked having this control. She could let the mistress go further, or she could stop it at any time. Yet as she glanced at their faces, it turned her on more to see such anticipation and lust in their eyes. Romeo signaled him over to the leather chair beside his so he could have a better view of the scene on the couch.

All she could hear was the slow sounds of London underground music in the background.

He watched as the mistress leaned in to kiss his girl. He licked his lips. Her hands were in constant motion on her, running her long, painted nails down her arms, up her legs, lingering around her breast area, lightly flickering over her nipples until they stood erect under her satin dress. Man he was glad she wore a dress tonight. His pants were throbbing already.

To his surprise, his girl leaned in to kiss back. She took the mistress's lips into her own soft lips, and he could almost feel the kiss himself. It was something he was all too familiar with. No one spoke a word, afraid to break the trance they all seemed to be in.

The mistress was now on her knees, her skirt hiked up revealing her lacy panties. She was kissing her thighs, running her tongue up her legs she pulled her legs further apart. Fully exposed, she could feel her juices slipping onto the couch. She had never thought she would enjoy this as much as she was, but she was thoroughly turned on, waiting for the mistress's next move, taking her breath away with every new touch. She allowed the mistress to penetrate her softness. There was something so different about a woman's touch. Softer. More erotic. Forbidden. And as she was being enjoyed, she watched Romeo and her rock star almost burst with jealousy and hunger. She moaned louder, adding to the ambiance, arching her back away from the couch and tilting her head back in exaggerated bliss.

Her breasts were left out the top of her dress that had been pulled down to expose her. The mistress had her hands around her hips, which had pushed up the dress from the bottom, exposing everything. Yet she didn't care. She knew they were all watching her, and it turned her on more. She enjoyed every touch, kiss, and lick of the tongue the mistress offered. But she needed more. She was on the verge of a substantial orgasm and wanted more, like she always did when she was this close. She squirmed around on that leather couch, now slippery with the juices of her and the mistress.

Her rock star came to her side and slid his fingers inside her. He kissed the mistress's lips, tasting her, and then went in for more of her. He circled his fingers around, driving her insane.

The mistress played with her clit, and Romeo came up behind his mistress and slid into her, pumping slowly at first so he could watch everything in front of him. He watched as his mistress and the rock star pleasured her. He reached around and slid his finger into her as well. "Put your finger in there too," he ordered his mistress.

She screamed from the sheer exotic pleasure of three people at one time. She flooded out, breathing heavily, and she watched as Romeo fucked the mistress as hard as he could. She and her Rock Star took turns kissing her. He sat on the couch, the mistress wrapping those magic hands of hers around the base of his member, stroking it up and down. He couldn't take anymore, so he pulled his girl on top of him, and she rode him fast and hard, then slow and easy, while the Mistress tasted them both.

She locked eyes with Romeo, and his smirk proved he just got what he wanted, like he always did.

She held his stare, daring him. And he may have taken her up on that offer, but he had nothing left. He fell forward on his mistress's back and heaved a sigh of exhaustion.

Rock 'N' Roll Confessions #13

The plane ride home was long and exhausting, and after a very long and exhausting weekend, she needed sleep. She pulled the sleep mask out of her carry on and slid it into place. Dreams and flashbacks tugged at her mind. She tried to block them out, but the haziness of sleep dragged them out of the corners of her mind. As she floated through the darkness toward sleep, images flashed faster and faster toward her unconscious mind.

She woke to find him on the bathroom floor, lying in his own vomit. Her head was pounding. How the hell did they get back to the hotel room?

"I need pills." The bright light of the bathroom was blinding her, sending piercing pain through her eyes.

"Hey, are you okay?" She pushed lightly at his side with her foot. Her voice was barely above a whisper.

Her body ached much like her head. And she used all the energy she had just to stand up. She needed to sit back down. He was still on the floor. Her mouth was so dry. *Water. I need water and pain pills.* She sat on the toilet, holding her head in her hands.

"Baby, wake up. I need something for my head." She had no energy left; she ran the cold water over a towel and lay on the floor beside him, placing the cool towel on her head. She fell back asleep.

Hours later she woke beside him, both of them half dressed. He hadn't moved. She rubbed the remnants of last night's make-up from her eyes. She squeezed them shut and opened them again to adjust to the white light of the bathroom. She noted dusk was peeking in through the curtains.

How long had they been there?

"Babe, we gotta get up. Come on. Get up." She leaned in to roll him over and noticed he was barely breathing, white foam dried at the corners of his mouth. Instantly, she fully awoke.

"OH MY GOD!" she screamed.

"HELP ME! Help me!" she cried.

"Baby get up, it's me. Come on, baby, come on." She smacked his face and tried to lift him off the floor.

She ran to the hallway and yelled for help. The concierge was on his way down the hall.

"Call 911! I need an ambulance!" she yelled through the hallway, hoping one of the band members were around. Doors opened and heads peeked out. Tears streaming down her face, she ran back to the bathroom. Sliding to the floor, she put his head in her lap. Rocking back and forth, she tried to wake him up. Nothing. His eyes remained rolled back, and his breath stayed short.

"Baby, you have to get up," she sobbed. "Don't leave me. Don't leave me. Don't leave me," she repeated over and over as she held him in her arms, rocking back and forth until the ambulance attendants arrived.

She didn't notice the band members or hotel staff that had come into the room. Vaguely somewhere in the distance she heard voices, hysteria, and someone say "overdose."

She jolted awake. She was still in the air, and the passenger beside her was laughing at the movie playing on the big screen at the front of the plane. She had no desire to laugh with the image of him laying on the floor still in her mind. She rubbed her forehead with the back of her hand and fell back into the unconsciousness of sleep.

With his stomach pumped and IVs in place to rehydrate him, she spoke with the doctors and the band members. He would be okay; it was a very close call. But the doctors were recommending rehab for him. The conversation quickly turned to aggravated accusations between the band members of who was going to stop him, how would they continue their tour, and everyone placing blame on someone else. She partly felt responsible as they asked about last night's events, half of which she had no recollection. She only remembered the mistress and Romeo, and she was not about to give them the dirty details of that. She had no idea of how they made it back to the hotel room. She left them to their arguments and peeked into the little rectangular window, allowing her a concealed view of him. Her heart ached at the sight of him with tubes and monitors coming out of his still body. She watched his stomach for the up and down movement of life. "Breathe, baby," she whispered to the window. She found herself breathing extra hard, as if trying to take breaths for him. Tears ran down her face, and she no longer heard the arguments of the band. She opened the door to his cold, sterile hospital room and walked in.

She was so tired. She lifted the covers and crawled in beside him, her arm around his waist to feel every breath. She cried to herself to sleep.

The plane was landing the next time she opened her tear-stained eyes. She packed up her little black carry on and buckled her seatbelt. She just wanted to be home. And she wanted him with her.

Rock 'N' Roll Confessions #14

She ran the water as hot as she could handle it, lit the lavender-scented candles, added lavender bubble bath, and breathed in a deep breath of relief. Happy to be home, she slid off her red satin robe, exposing her body to the steam-filled air. She dipped her toe in to test the water; steam floated up, relaxing her that much more. The water was hot, probably too hot, but she slid in anyway, stopping halfway to let her body adjust to the temperature of the water. She breathed in deep and lowered herself in, feeling her skin turn pink. She laid her head back on the blow-up pillow and let her body and mind fully relax. She could feel the tensions of the weekend wash away. She had just received the latest update on him. He was still sleeping a lot, which he probably needed. Given the lifestyle he'd been living the last few months, it was bound to catch up to him. She just wished she didn't feel partly responsible, and she desperately wanted to get the image of him lying on the bathroom floor out of her head. She had never been so scared in her life. She soaked the terrycloth in the hot water, wrung it out, and placed it over her face to breathe in the steam, feeling the tears fill up in her eyes. A thought crossed her mind; she was falling in love with him. "No," she thought out loud. "It's just the events of the weekend taking its toll on you." She was talking to herself. Great, now she was in love and crazy! "Empty your mind, empty your mind." She repeated over and over to try to clear her mind and send her into a state of meditation.

Her mind did start to wander, as did her hands. She hadn't even realized it, but she was rubbing her hand across her breast, circling to the other and then down to her tummy. The bubbles were rising over the edge of the tub; she lifted her leg to tame some of them down and checked the smoothness of her legs by running her hand from her ankle up. She was soft. With that thought in mind, it brought on images of the mistress touching her legs with her long, painted nails. She felt a drop in her tummy and a stirring inside. She let her hand continue up her own leg, mimicking the mistress's moves, running down the other long, lean leg and back up again. She felt her face flush red—from the heat of the water or the thought of the mistress, she wasn't sure. Her mind flashed to the moment he was inside her and the mistress was pleasuring them both. Her stomach dropped.

She let her hand roam her chest and belly while the other ventured south. Separating her lips with her fingers allowed the hot water to rush in and the tingle begin in her toes. The tingle that led up her legs as she played with herself and her mind played with more images of the mistress. Her heart rate quickened, her bicep tensing, and she saw another flash of the mistress's lips. Her kisses were sweet—different than a man's kiss, so much softer. Her temperature was rising, as was the feeling within her. Her entire body was now tense, and the images of sex were flashing insanely fast through her mind. Red lips and red nails—she licked her own lips with the thought of the mistress's lips on her. She was secretly wishing the mistress was here with her right now to take her to her climax with her magical tongue. Her heart rate quickened, and her fingers played faster and faster. Her back arched, lifting her body forward as she climaxed. She moaned loudly and sighed, falling back on the blow-up pillow; the water splashed up behind her, wetting her hair. She submersed her head under the still-steaming water and let it wash away the stress of the weekend.

Rock 'N' Roll Confessions #15

Another city, another show.

Almost a year had passed since the overdose, and they were still partying just as hard. She was visiting him for a week this time and was hoping to get some real alone time with him. She had made a point of visiting him more often on the road in hopes of taking better care of him. The hospital stint had not been enough to put a hold on the partying for him or anyone else in the band. The band members preached for about the first month or so, but when he had blown up and refused rehab, they just gave up. He insisted he didn't have a problem, and although everyone else thought different, it didn't stop them from continuing to party with him—herself included. They were young, famous, and invincible. He was a growing concern of hers, and she was torn between staying and leaving.

The sight of him on the floor weighed heavy on her mind. And that's what kept her coming around. She was growing tired of the tour life, even though she only visited from time to time. She had noticed in the last year a huge difference in his attitude and personality. His ego and show persona had started to peek through into his offstage life, and she didn't like it too much. She much preferred the dark, mysterious lover he used to be before all this. Now it seemed he was all about himself and his name, something she could live without. Even with all that, she was still very excited to see him.

She walked into the bar to meet up with him for a drink before heading to the hotel room. She stopped at the entrance; her eyes searched the crowded room, and a table of guys sitting close by stared with their open mouths. "You can sit here, sexy!" one of the braver ones said. The others just stared. She knew she looked hot. She always made a point of dressing extra sexy on the days she saw him.

And as if by cue, he walked up to her and stopped dead. He had a strange look on his face. "You made it," was all he said.

"Yes, I did." She noticed something different about him instantly. Was he stoned? He reached up and hugged her half-assed. She put her arms around him, and he patted her on the back. *Well, that was a new one,* she said in her mind.

"Umm, okay, come on back to the table."

She didn't like the way he was acting. Something was definitely up. When she got to the table, she noticed a few girls at the table with the band, which, in all honesty, she told herself, was not a big deal. What was a big deal was the girl that scorned her look of evil as she shifted over to the next chair.

Who is this bitch? she thought and almost said out loud.

"Are you fucking high?" she whispered in his ear.

"No, baby. Come here, sit with me." He kissed her sloppily half on the mouth, half on the cheek.

"Look, if you're … involved with something or *someone*, I can leave." She wouldn't sit down; she just stared back at the bitch giving her the evil eye. Obviously she was interrupting something. She figured out right away that this one was not with anyone else in the band but him. Everyone else seemed awfully quiet all of a sudden. She stood her ground and stared that bitch right in the eye. She generally was not the jealous type, and had no room to be, really. She knew he slept with other girls. Or at least she wasn't dumb enough to believe that he wasn't sleeping with other girls when she was not around. She herself had slept with a few on the side. She even had another rendezvous with the mistress and Romeo that he had no idea about. It was an unspoken rule between them. They just didn't talk about the other affairs. They weren't a couple, she reminded herself. But this was just plain rude.

And to invite her here while this skank was with him? Well this might be the last fucking straw!

"Come on, sit down, have a drink. How've you been?" He sat down and crossed his legs ridiculously, placing his elbow on his knee, and flicked his hand.

"Who the fuck are you?" she blurted out. This was just outrageous! He was definitely on something, and the bitch had something to do with it. She looked just as fried as he did, and she was still staring her down. She could feel the glare through the back of her head.

"Who the fuck are you?" Bitch snarled from behind her.

"Oh, girls, come on now, no cat fights needed here." His words were slurred, and the more she heard his voice, the more she wanted to slap the stupidity right out of him.

She whipped her head around and viciously answered, "You obviously don't know who I am, or you wouldn't be asking, so I will give you the benefit of the doubt and explain it to you. *I*, unlike you, am not a groupie whore. *I* am a long-time friend of his, and that is all you need to know. So get out of my face before you make the biggest mistake of your life." She could feel the heat of anger rising in her body, starting at her toes and filling her stomach with that gut-wrenching rage that made her blind with madness.

The bitch open-handedly smacked her in the face. She didn't feel the sting on her cheek right away. What she did feel was her hands around the bitch's neck, as she was all of a sudden on top of her as the girl gasped for air on the floor. The guys tried to pull her off and break up the fight.

When she finally let go of the girl on the floor, she stood up. "Let go of me. I don't need you to settle me down. I'm fine."

"Baby, what'd you do that for? She was just hanging out with me. You're never here, and she is …" His speech slurred. She did not like who he was right now or who he was becoming. He stepped over the girl on the floor and came to her, trying to smooth his way into her.

He was so fucked up right now. The anger in her boiled again. "I'm never here? That's all you have to say? I don't …"

"Baby …" she cut him off and waved her hand in his face.

"I don't care what you do when I'm not around. I do my own thing too. What I do care about is coming here after I've taken time out of my life for you and finding some crack whore, sitting at the table that I am supposed to be having dinner at with YOU!"

He stood there dumbfounded; he knew when she was this angry to shut up. As messed up as he was right now, he knew to just shut up. He saw her eyes turn that wicked shade of green and knew. He also knew when she was this mad, no one could calm her down but herself. And that was only after she said what she had to say. The band knew it as well and stood there with their heads down. Not one of them could look her in the eye.

"I'm done with you! I'm *so* fucking done with you. You have it all, and you're too fucking high to realize it! So you know what? End up like all of your idols, dead from an overdose before you're thirty years old. I don't give a shit anymore. You'd think you would've learned last year!" Everyone in the bar was staring at them, and she was sure this would end up in some tabloid magazine by the morning, but she didn't care anymore. She wanted, no needed, him to hear all the things that had been eating her up all year.

"You think you're so great? You should see yourself right now. Your ego and head have grown so big I don't think there's enough room in here for both of them! And you want to know what I see? I see," she stopped. "I see." Her arms had been flailing everywhere as she yelled at him, but she stopped, lowered her arms and her voice, and simply said, "Nothing."

She turned on her heels, red, his favorite color, and walked away, but not before she saw the devastation in his face. If someone could sober up in one minute, he just had.

Rock 'N' Roll Confessions #16

Sitting in the airport lobby, she replayed the day's events in her head. She had only herself to blame. She had allowed herself to fall for him, to let it become more than it was in her mind and her heart. Her eyes still ached from her earlier tears. She made a promise to herself never to cry over him again. She no longer wanted to see him, talk to him, or have anything else to do with him. Who was she fooling, thinking she could fix him? He had some serious drug addictions going on, and there was nothing anyone could do for him. He had to fix himself, and until he did, she was writing him out of her life.

She kept her sunglasses on to hide the redness of her eyes in the airport and sat beside the large glass windows pretending to stare out into the sun-filled day.

Her feet were beginning to ache from the four-inch pointy-toed spikes she'd had on all day. The thought that she had worn them for him was making her feet ache more, and she wanted nothing more than to throw them across the room right now.

Her little black dress was all of a sudden too tight; she felt her chest tighten with it. She felt the need to move around before she drove herself crazy with thoughts of him. And he wasn't worth another minute of her time.

Adjusting the hem on her dress, she strolled rather quickly toward the little coffee shop to grab a bite to eat. Because she had been in her own world with her mind on everything but walking, she walked right into a tall, dark, handsome man.

"I'm sorry," she muttered and continued on.

"I know you," he said.

She knew the voice, had heard it before, so turned to see the face that matched it.

There stood Romeo, looking devilishly sexy, his dark eyes immediately recognizing her.

"How are you, Princess? Coming in or going out?" he asked and secretly hoped she was going out and not coming in to see that wreck of a rock star. Sure, he had talent, but the talk around him lately was all drugs, booze, and women. And this fireball in front of him deserved more.

"Oh, going out. I'm good, though, you?" It was the first time she had ever seen him alone. It felt a little awkward; she had only known him sexually, in the dark hours of night with other erotic elements and people.

"So am I. Going home? I could give you a lift." She actually laughed at his comment.

"Yes, I'm going home. Bad day, and I'm exhausted. But I'm on standby. I wasn't supposed to leave for another week." She tried not to explain as she explained.

"What do you mean, you could give me a lift? You driving to Canada, or do you have your own plane?" she laughed and said with a smirk. That wicked little smile made him melt.

Her every movement left him yearning for her. She had so much more than any other girl he had met. He often thought of her, even though it had been almost a year since the last time he saw her.

"No, I don't have a plane. I have a personal jet. And I would be happy to give you a lift to Toronto. Close enough. I have business to tend to there."

She laughed on the verge of hysteria. "You're kidding, right?" She wondered how much money this guy actually had.

"No, I'm serious. Although, if you want to stay here and wait for a standby flight you are more than welcome to; I, on the other hand, have to get going." He didn't really have to leave for another hour, but he liked throwing his money and power around this one. He felt the need to impress her. It was a very hard task indeed.

"You're damn right I'm coming!" She needed this crazy distraction. And it would probably be the only time she would ever see the inside of a private jet. Come to think of it, this would be the only time she would know someone with their own private jet. *Crazy fucking day, might as well roll with it,* she told herself. He pulled her sleek black suitcase for her, and they headed out to board the jet. She mildly felt guilty for leaving with him. She knew he would mad if he knew she was going on Romeo's jet. He'd be mad if he knew she talked to him without him around. Well, the person he used to be would've been mad. Who knows what this new persona would do. And she suddenly didn't care anymore as the image of that trashy bitch came to mind.

She sat back in the tan suede and leather bucket seat on his jet. Who could fly any other way after this? Thoroughly enjoying the moment, she kicked off her heels to fully relax.

"Oh, that feels so much better," she said aloud. He handed her a champagne glass.

"Enjoy. I find I enjoy it much more when someone comes on for the first time." He sat across from her in the other seat. "Here, give me your foot." He motioned for her to place a foot in his lap

"Yeah, right." She threw her head back and laughed.

"No, really. Give me your foot. You look like you could use a good foot rub. I don't know how you girls wear those things!" He wanted to rub more than her foot. She was so beautiful, wicked looking really; bewitching in a sense.

"Well, if you insist." She raised her long leg and placed a foot in his lap. He immediately picked it up and began to massage it.

"Oh, now this I could get used to." Drink in hand, massage, private jet. She felt like she was in some weird movie or twilight zone.

"So, your friend, the rock star?"

"Oh, don't mention him please. That's the reason I'm on my way home. Well actually, you are the reason I'm on my home. He's the reason I was waiting for a standby in the airport." She felt herself tensing up again, so she took another sip of her champagne.

"So then you know he needs to straighten himself out," he plainly put.

"Yes, I do. Unfortunately, he doesn't. I really don't want to talk about this. Can we not?"

"Of course. You sit back and enjoy the ride." He picked up her other foot and began to massage it.

"That's more like it," she said and gave him one of her winning smiles that made any man melt, this one seeming much easier than any other.

He wanted to touch her smooth legs. Those legs went on for miles, and he knew where they led—somewhere else he wanted to go.

He refrained from coming on to strong. He didn't want to scare her away. What he really wanted was to win her over, keep her for himself for a long time, and mostly, he wanted to take her away from the rock star. He always found a way to get what he wanted. The trouble was, he didn't know quite how to get it this time. How do you make someone look at you the way they looked at each other? Sure, they may put on a good front of an open relationship, but he saw the rock star's need for her. It grew deep inside him; he just didn't know how to keep it. She was different, though. He could tell she could turn off her switch in a heartbeat, and he didn't want that to happen here with him. He was planning to play the knight in shining armor, here to rescue her. He also knew that she was not the type that wanted to be seen as needing to be rescued. She held a very strong wall around her, and he was sure she didn't let anyone over that wall. That's why the rock star was left behind and she was on her way home with him. He had to play his cards right with her. He felt that need growing inside him, a need he didn't understand himself, much like any other man that encountered this vixen; the vibe she carried around herself was bewitching. He doubted she knew what she did to men—and women. His last mistress fell for her just as hard as he had. She was always bringing her up and begging him to get in touch with her. It was one of the reasons they parted ways. After their last encounter, he realized he wanted her for himself. As intoxicating as it was to have two gorgeous women at one time, this one was more than enough for anyone. And he was not the sharing type. He took what he wanted, when he wanted. A little flash of the green was usually enough to lure any girl in, yet he knew money meant nothing to this one. She liked the musician type, and most of them come from nothing, like her rock star. She had stayed with him for so long, so that was a sure sign that money would not impress her. He did own the record company her rock star was signed on with, that one along with several others. Should he play that card? He pondered so many thoughts while he held her long, slender foot in his hand, his fingers sliding over each tiny bone, the softness of her skin warming under his touch. Oh how he wanted to touch more of her. Venturing a little further to her ankles, he made slow, circular movements over the pointy bones on the side of her ankles; a quick run up her shins, her skin melted under his hands, feeling more of silk than skin. Never had he felt skin so soft in his life. Gently he squeezed her calf muscles as his hands circled around her legs. She fell further in the chair, sliding slightly forward, pushing her foot into his groin.

"Oh, sorry." She laughed. "Guess I got a little too relaxed there."

"Not a problem. You're supposed to be relaxing. Didn't you have a bad day?" he asked in hopes of her revealing the day's incidents. Mind you, he knew that if it was a public display, he'd hear about it soon enough.

"Oh yeah," was all she said. Her thoughts had drifted away from the day's events, and she didn't want to think about them anymore. It was done, over, and she was just starting to enjoy his company.

"You were massaging, remember?" She pushed at his groin with her foot. He continued to rub her legs and pushed up further.

"Can I kiss you?" he whispered, as if he didn't really want her to hear his question. Keeping his head low, he shifted his eyes upward to meet hers.

"I don't know, can you?" she teased.

He let her feet fall to the floor and went down on his knees; with both hands on the arms of the chairs, he kissed her softly. She pulled his bottom lip in between hers and suckled it.

"You have to be the sexiest girl I've ever met," he admitted.

"I know." His hand traced up her arm and slid the strap of her dress off her shoulder. Leaning in to kiss her shoulder, he felt himself growing with anticipation. She lifted a leg and wrapped it around his waist.

"Take your shirt off," she ordered him in that sultry voice of hers.

He immediately obeyed, exposing his bare chest to her, and he felt strangely naked. Not naked in the lack of clothing sense; it was different. He was at her mercy.

She leaned forward and ran her hands over his arms, moving up to his shoulders and running her palms down over his chest.

"Kiss me." Another order from her, and all he could do was obey and wait for his next command. He wondered when she took control and how he allowed her to.

She ordered him gently, figuring it was his thing, knowing about his mistress obsession. But she would make it very clear that she would never be one of his mistresses. This was just revenge sex for her. Good revenge sex. But revenge nonetheless. She wished with every touch, every kiss, that Mr. Rock Star would feel it. She wanted him to hear her every moan and cry.

She stood so her dress would fall to the floor, exposing her body. She watched him kneeling on the floor at her feet, awaiting her next command. "Touch me. I know you want to." She spoke calmly, quietly.

His hands wandered over every inch of her body, followed by his lips, then his tongue. He picked her up and carried her over to the couch, laid her on her back, and let his tongue work magic on her. Finally he was the one tasting her. Not the rock star. Not the mistress. He didn't have to share her this time.

She exaggerated every movement, every arch of her back, and when she finally reached her climax, she squealed extra loud in hopes that he could feel it. Hear it. She raked her nails down Romeo's back, leaving red welts; she dug her nails in his ass, leaving as many marks as she could; her body felt Romeo, but her heart and her mind felt the rock star. And she hoped that he felt her hands, digging into another man.

Sweat poured over their naked bodies, and he slid in and out of her, enjoying every thrust. She urged him for more. "Satisfy me," she whispered, desperately hoping he could feed the hunger in her. He was eager to please her, to satisfy her, but he sensed she was trying to satisfy more than her sexual fantasies. He gave her everything he had, and when he couldn't fuck her anymore, he lifted her up onto the back of the small couch, spreading her legs, and gave her more than he had left. He explored deeply with his fingers, twisting and turning, making her squirm, and still she called for more. Her hands were on his head. He felt his power unfold; she made him feel needed. He felt more of a man than he had ever felt. That was her thing. That's what her power was.

Exhausted, she slid back down the couch, and he fell beside her. Her body was fully relaxed.

After the jet had landed, he had a car waiting for her to take her home. Hell, she could get used to this kind of life. They exchanged phone numbers; he would be in town for a few weeks on business and wanted to meet up with her again. *No harm in that,* she thought. She rather enjoyed the flight home; they had great conversation and great sex.

She walked into her apartment, threw her keys on the side table, and noticed her answering machine blinking. Twenty messages; she didn't have the energy to listen to them now. She knew who most of them would be from. She brought her bags to her room, dropped them on the floor, and fell onto her bed and slept.

Rock 'N' Roll Confessions #17

Crazy, absurd dreams flooded her sleep. She tossed and turned as she dreamt of the airplane falling apart, pieces of the floor falling through the sky. He was beside her, and she was yelling at him to sit down and put his seatbelt on. He wouldn't listen to her. He was yelling, "I can fly!" She was in hysterics, realizing he was high and hallucinating. He fell through a hole in the floor, and she screamed as he fell down, farther and farther away from her. She couldn't save him. She woke to her own screams, and tears flooded her face. She hugged her knees tight to her chest and rocked back and forth.

She got up and slid out of her dress, reached into her armoire, and pulled out her lounge pants and tank top. Once she was dressed, she walked barefoot to the kitchen, reached into the fridge, and grabbed a beer. Before leaving the kitchen, she finished the beer and grabbed another one. She'd need more than one to listen to those messages.

Sitting on the chair beside the answering machine, she contemplated pressing the play button. Did she really want to hear anything he had to say? Did something bad happen to him? She finished the second beer, got up and grabbed two more, and pressed play.

The first few messages were from friends wishing her well on her trip, with plans to get together when she returned. What a waste that was! One was from a telemarketer. She hit delete before she even finished listening to that one.

The next fifteen were from him. The first was, "Baby, it's me. I hope you didn't go home. But I called the hotel and they said you never checked in. I'm worried about you. Please call me. You know she doesn't mean anything. Don't be like this. Who's my girl?" Beep. His voice was still in that slow, stoned tone that made her roll her eyes and down the rest of beer number three.

Message number two, beer number four. "Okay, I'm still looking for you. I can't find you anywhere. Just come to my hotel room, and we'll make up, okay, baby? Come on, I know you're not still mad. Did you go home? Please tell me where you are. I'm worried. Call me." Beep.

She couldn't believe he was acting like not much had happened. He must've been so fucking high that he didn't even remember the scene in the bar or restaurant or wherever they had been. She didn't remember much

90

of it herself, something that happened through rage. That was no excuse, she told herself. She was done with him. She contemplated listening to the rest of the messages.

The next few messages were basically him repeating himself. I'm sorry. Where are you? Blah, blah, blah. The last three were totally different, starting with the one that broke her heart and almost broke her down to call him back.

"Baby," he sobbed. "I'm so fucked up! I don't know what's wrong with me. I need help. I know that." She could hear the tears in his voice. "I can't do this without you. I need you. I need you here with me, all the time. I need *you*. This life is hard. So fucking hard." He paused with torment in his words.

"Come back to me. Just you and me, babe. I'll go to rehab. I'll do whatever it takes. I'll stop touring for a while, get my shit together; no more women, no more drugs." Another long pause followed by sobbing words, "I'm so sorry. I'm so fucking sorry. I love you." Beep. He got cut off. She sat there with tears rolling down her cheeks and the phone in her hand. She was just about to call him when the next message started.

"FUCK YOU! You don't want me? I don't fucking care anymore either! You BITCH! I pour my heart out to you, and you can't even call me? FUCK YOU! I don't need you, or anyone else!" She heard him snort the next line up his nose and then heard him smash something against the wall. "Don't call me. I don't want you to. I don't want to see you anymore. You don't want me, well you know what? There's plenty of woman that do! There's one here right now. Listen, can you hear her?" He laughed a very malicious laugh that left her shaking and enraged. And that was why she was done. She immediately erased her entire answering machine, not wanting to hear the rest.

Rock 'N' Roll Confessions #18

The black car was out front of her house waiting to pick her up to take her to the airport, and she was running behind. She had been seeing Romeo for more than six months, and it was going well. They were heading out to LA for the awards show. She was definitely enjoying the perks that came with him. She hadn't heard from her rock star since the night of nasty, as she referred to it. Nor did she want to. She still thought about him all the time but had no desire to see him. He hadn't tried to contact her, so why should she try to get in touch with him?

She threw the last few items into her bag and ran out the door. He opened the door for her. "Hello, Princess." His usual greeting, followed by a kiss on the mouth.

"Hey! Sorry I'm running late. I had a crazy day and fell behind." She hurried her words as she jumped in the car.

"Well, you're here now, and we're on our way to LA. What could be better than that?" His stomach still dropped at the sight of her. Even standing there in her jeans and tee shirt, she looked hot. He had a big surprise for her this weekend that he couldn't wait to give to her. He was worried about the awards show; the rock star was going to be there. His band had been nominated for several awards. He hoped he was still a mess, that way his Princess wouldn't give a shit. He was secretly keeping her away from the rock star, but with the awards show, they all had to be there. And he did want that asshole to see her walking arm in arm with him. The rock star had tried to call her a few times, left her messages of how sorry he was and how he needed to see her. But Romeo just erased those before she even heard them. He knew he was playing with fire. If she ever found out, she would kick his ass to the curb. He rationalized his behavior; she didn't need someone like that in her life. She needed someone like himself, who could take care of her, buy her anything she wanted, and he meant anything. He already flew her out to the Islands for a week. Bottom line was, he wanted to keep her away from the rock star. He wanted to win. He was in a male ego battle with the rock star and had been since the first night they met. After that night, the rock star had called him and told him to stay away from his girl. Well, whose girl was she now? His, and he intended to keep it that way. She, of course, knew nothing of this. She would kill them both if she ever found out that she was sought after as a prize.

She sat in the car looking out the window, with all her thoughts on her rock star. She knew he was going to be at the awards. He was nominated, and she really wanted him to win. She was worried that he was going to be there with some tramp when she should've been the one by his side for one of the biggest moments of his life. The thought frustrated her. Why did he have to fuck up such a good thing? The last few months had been adventurous, great at times, but something wasn't there. Something was missing. He wasn't a boyfriend, even though she knew he thought of them as a couple. She was not the couple type and had explained this to him. He had responded with, "Call it what you will, I don't care." But he did. She knew that he was starting to get serious with her, so she was trying to back off and would be missing in action a lot more once they returned from LA.

"Where'd you go?" he asked.

"What? Oh, sorry; guess I got lost in my thoughts. Just going over the day's work. Am I ever happy we're heading out of town. I need it." She tried to chalk her quietness up to her day at work.

"I think you need a distraction." He flirted with the hopes of having her in the car right now. He reached between her legs.

Defensively, her legs crossed. She didn't mean to. It just happened.

"What is that about?" He sat back, shocked. She was always in the mood.

"Sorry, just tired. Maybe I should nap on the way so I'm refreshed for tonight."

"Ok, Princess, lay back, have a nap, so later we can indulge!" He laughed as he raised his eyebrows repeatedly.

She shook her head and giggled, "You're nuts." He was very sexy. Dark hair, dark eyes, wicked body, gave her everything—so why wasn't she feeling it? Maybe she was just tired.

They stepped out of the jet into a wall of humid heat. The heaviness of it hit her in the chest. She tried to take a deep breath, "How fuckin' hot is it here today?"

"Not as hot as you. Now you know how I feel every day!" His cheesy line made her smile and shake her head.

"Crazy," was her only response. She wrapped her arm around his waist, putting her hand in his back pocket.

Rock 'N' Roll Confessions #19

She slid into her long, black evening gown, the slit reaching her hip bone. *No panties tonight,* she thought. The back of her dress was a low swoop of material, exposing the small of her back and the top of her ass. One wrong movement and she would be completely exposed, but damn she looked sexy from every angle. Even the front of her dress was low cut. Black stilettos embraced her slender feet, elongating her leg even more. She stepped out of the room with her hair swept up in a messy swirl, make-up on, and the dress that would make every man fall at her feet.

He was speechless. He knew she was hot, but this, this was beyond hot. She would stop people in the tracks on the red carpet tonight.

"Sweet fuck!"

"You like?" She laughed.

"Understatement of the year. Okay, back in the bedroom, we're not going anywhere!" She laughed again.

"Oh yes we are! This dress has to be seen! Besides, you bought the dress; you should've known how it would look!" she teased him but thoroughly enjoyed this surprise.

"Well, yes. I knew you would look smokin' hot in it. But I can't even begin to describe how you look! Worth every cent!" He stood with his mouth wide open.

"Well, how much was it?" she asked, knowing it was probably a small fortune.

"You really want to know?"

"No, probably not. It'll make me nervous to wear it. But okay, tell me!"

"Twenty-five thousand." He knew it was too much for a dress, but he wanted her to be the talk of the night, and he wanted that rock star to kick himself in the ass when he saw her, and with him. He could already sense the jealousy.

"Fuck off! Now I can't wear it! Oh, I knew I shouldn't have asked! Why did you tell me?" She panicked. Now she would worry all night about the dress.

"You asked. That's why I told you. And don't worry. If it gets ruined, I'll get you another one!"

"Now I know you're crazy! Come on Mr. Millions! Let's get our asses there already!" She kissed him hard on the lips and pulled at his hand.

Romeo flooded her with complements on the ride over; he couldn't keep his hands off her. He was running his hand up the length of her smooth legs, finding nothing under the dress.

"You're not wearing any panties." He wanted her right there in the car.

"No, I'm not and I'm not wearing a bra either. Just me under this very expensive dress!" Her stomach was doing flips for more than one reason. One wrong move and everyone would know she wasn't wearing anything under this fabulous dress. She was planning her escape from the car without incident. That's all she needed was to be exposed on the front page of every tabloid magazine in the country.

"I want to fuck you right now!" His manhood was throbbing in his tux pants, sliding around the silk material of his underwear—he was wearing some. But it wasn't helping him any. The silk only made matters worse. There was something about the way if felt slipping around in there. It reminded him of a woman's touch.

"Oh, I'm not ruining this dress, my hair, or anything else. You'll have to wait. So behave yourself!" The wetness between her legs was telling him otherwise.

"But it feels so nice and warm in there. Let me touch you, just a little." His voice lowered into that tone of sexual urgency.

"No, be good."

"Oh, I'll be good all right! I'll be six times good."

"Are you promising me six orgasms? Because I'll hold you to that; just not now. You'll have to wait till later tonight. And what will the limo driver think?"

"First of all, who cares. I'm sure he's seen it all. Second, later is REALLY later. We have the awards show and then the after party, which I'm hosting, so we have to go to. Hell, it'll be morning before we get to fuck." He was still playing his way in there. "Just let me have a taste, nothing more; just enough to hold me off, till later." His head was between her legs before she could answer.

"That feels so good. But you've had enough!" She pushed his head away with both hands. Wow, he really wanted her tonight. And if it weren't for the dress, she would have let him have all of her. Suddenly she was in the mood.

"Look, we're here. Get up. And wipe your mouth." She was really nervous now.

He stepped out of the car first, reached in, and took her by the hand to lead her out onto the red carpet. Cameras flashed everywhere, blinding them. She smiled, not for the cameras as much as getting out of the car without incident.

She carried herself with more confidence than she ever had. The excitement of the evening was heavy in the air, and she couldn't help but get caught up in it herself.

Being escorted down the long aisle, she focused on not falling over on her spiky heels and not falling out of her dress. His arm was wrapped tightly around her waist; she noticed he hadn't left her side since they arrived, stopping to chat with this one and that one. Congratulating people on their nominations and wishing them luck for the evening.

One foot in front of the other, her hips swayed from side to side, her leg fully exposed as she took each step. They reached the aisle they would be sitting in, and when she turned to sit down, her heart stopped. He was two aisles back, right behind them. He looked up at her with a sparkle in his eye, and then he saw Romeo. And all he saw was red. Instantly, he thought, *I'll make him pay for bringing her.*

She sat very still in her seat, every so often, trying to turn her head to catch a glimpse at him. She knew he was staring at her the entire time. She could feel his eyes burning through the back of her head. The thought made her uncomfortable—the thought that he was right behind her on his biggest night and she wasn't beside him, where she should be. Instead she was here with Romeo. It didn't seem right.

The category for his first nomination was up next, and she was on pins and needles for him; her stomach was turning with anticipation.

He sat stiff, afraid to move, desperately hoping the band would win at least one if not all the awards they were up for. He didn't want to lose in front of her. Or fucking Romeo. Why the hell was she here with him? Every muscle in his body held anger over the sight of them together. He had told Romeo to stay away from her.

"Hey, did you know they were together?" he leaned over and whispered in the drummer's ear.

"Yeah. Sorry man, we didn't know how to tell you. It happened while you were in rehab. I didn't know they would be here together, or else we would've told you. Shake it off. Man, we are about to win some fuckin' awards here!" He patted him on the knee.

"The winner is …" they both held their breath.

She didn't hear the name the presenter had called, but she knew they had won from the screams and whistles coming from behind her. Her eyes filled with tears, and she stood up and turned to look at him in his moment of glory. Applauding him, she was too late to see them jump up out of their seats, but she felt a hand on her arm pulling at her.

She didn't have enough time to realize what was going on, when her rock star pulled her close to him and kissed her hard on the mouth. Romeo's face dropped.

He pulled her up onto the stage with him and the band. Fuck, she looked smokin' hot. He was gonna get her back. She was his. And that would never change.

"Oh," squeaked out of her mouth.

She was beaming with pride for her friends on stage—for him, for the band, and for where they came from. Never did she imagine standing in front of millions of people wearing a twenty-five thousand dollar dress, standing beside him while he accepted his award wearing ripped jeans, a tee shirt, a tux jacket, and a tie loosely knotted.

"You did it, baby," she whispered in his ear. They shouted out their thanks to the crowd, rock on hands in the air, pats on the back, hugs all around. He never once let her hand go. He picked her up and swung her around in a circle before they left the stage.

"Ah My dress!" She squealed, afraid of losing something or everything out of the dress.

"Oh, we'll talk about that later! You sexy bitch!" He was on cloud nine. His girl was in his arms, and the band had just won their first award of the night.

Followed by three others.

She forgot about Romeo while she was on the stage and now realized how awkward it would be going back to sit down beside him.

"What the hell was that about?" he asked with a winning smile but malevolence in his voice.

"What? That? Oh, they were just excited. I've known them for years. Used to sit in the garage and freeze my ass off while they practiced. Guess they thought I should be there with them. Don't worry." She patted him lightly on the leg, a gesture he found too general.

Rock 'N' Roll Confessions #20

They arrived at the after-hours party, Romeo seeming unusually distant and cranky. Yet he wouldn't take his arms or his eyes off her.

She was beginning to feel like his trophy, and it was getting on her nerves, making her cranky.

"Are you still upset about what happened at the show?" she finally asked once they had a moment to themselves.

"No. Why, should I be? Just because my girlfriend went in front of everyone I could possibly know and kissed another guy? Why should I be upset about that?" Obviously he was.

"I already explained that to you. Really, give it up. I'm not going to have you sulking all night. It's a big turn off." She turned her head away from him, noticing the waiter with a tray of champagne. She reached for a glass.

"A big turn off, is it? And kissing someone else is not a big turn off for me? Look, you came here with me, and you're leaving with me!" The nastiness was coming out in his voice.

"I am NOT your property! So don't treat me like I am! We're ending this conversation right now before we both say something we can't take back!"

"You're right. We'll talk about this later in private." He reached his hand out to shake someone's hand and started up a conversation with him.

Before he could introduce her, she took the opportunity to break away, wanting to find him; he had to be here. It was his label throwing the party.

She moved through the crowd like a panther on the prowl for its next meal. Her green eyes searching the crowd, she felt as strong and sexy as a panther. She knew every man in the place was following every curve of her body as she sauntered through, grabbing more champagne from the waiters as she passed them. Where was he?

She finally stumbled across him, sitting in a corner his head hung low. He was here alone. He had no date. He looked more like himself, and it was nice to see. His huge ego had gone, even though this night he earned it. She appreciated seeing him for what he used to be.

"Hey, stranger." She stood with her legs slightly apart, hand on hip, the other holding her champagne. Her sultry voice was inviting him back. His hair was shorter, shoulder length. It suited him.

"Hey, baby. Thanks for coming," he said with that sexy tone that made her melt.

"Thanks for coming? That's it?" She sat beside him.

"Can we go talk somewhere quiet?" He lacked any emotion, which made it hard to read where this was going.

"Of course." They walked outside onto the grounds gardens. "Are you okay? You seem different."

"You're driving me fucking crazy! That dress, those shoes! Your hair! The way you smell." He had stopped walking. He touched both of her arms with his hands, squeezing her as he moved his hands up to her shoulders.

"Really, fucking killin' me here!" His voice was low and intense. He pushed her up against the garden wall and kissed her passionately, running his hands down the opening in the back of her dress. There was nothing to this dress, just material draped over the important parts. The dress screamed, "Undress me!"

And that's exactly what he wanted to do. Her skin felt like liquid fire under his hands, his insides burning with lust and greed. She was his, and he wanted her back.

He traced feather touches on every inch of exposed skin. Kissing her, he held her against the wall. His groin was pulsing. "I need you. I need you now. Here," he begged.

"I need you too," she whispered back, her insides quivering with anticipation, her legs weakening. She ran her hands through his hair. She loved touching his head, winding the hair around her fingers. He savored every touch, kiss, and taste, taking his time, even though it was killing him to go slow. He wanted to take her in his arms and ram his cock so hard into her that she'd stop breathing. His hand slid into the side of her dress, finding warm liquid. She was ready and eager too. He'd make her suffer, the way he'd been suffering for the last six months without her.

Sliding one finger in and out, circling her pleasure spot and back in again with two, slowly pulling them out and circling, then three, nice and slow. Speeding up as her heart rate quickened.

She was panting and whispering, "Take me now. Take me now." She grasped frantically at his belt, trying to pull it off, fumbling she managed to pull out his hard muscle, stroking quickly. She lifted her leg around his waist, her juices flowing freely.

He rammed it into her. Pinning her against the wall, he took no mercy on her. Fast and hard. Aggressively reclaiming what was his. She had both legs around his waist, and he was holding her up against the wall, her arms around his neck, holding on for dear life. Thrusting deeper with each stroke, she could feel the scratchy cement of the garden wall scraping at the exposed skin on her back. She cried out, "NOW! Now. NOW!"

"No, not now. Ride it out, baby." She thrust her hips back and forth over his long, hard member. They kissed passionately, her hands tangled in his sweaty hair, his hands holding her up by her ass.

"I missed you," she hushed.

"Me too, baby. Me too. Now. NOW!" He was about to cum and wanted to leave her shaking as well.

"Yes. Yes. Yes," she replied.

He fell forward with her in his arms and leaned against the garden wall. Her head was nuzzled into his hair, and she kissed his neck. His pants were around his ankles, and her dress was hiked up from her legs being wrapped around his waist. Raw, dirty sex. That was their thing. She was completely satisfied for the first time in months. Only him. Only he could do it.

They stayed in each other's arms, standing in the middle of the garden, fully exposed, afraid to let go of each other. They were breathing heavy, not saying a word.

A solo applause echoed through the night. "Very, well, done." Romeo hissed as he applauded and walked toward them.

Rock 'N' Roll Confessions #21

All they could do was stare at him. It's not like he hadn't seen what had just happened. *How did this happen?* she thought to herself. The same way it always happened with him, it just did. She lowered her legs, and her dress fell down, covering her back up. She almost laughed at the sight of him pulling his pants up in the middle of a garden. But given the circumstances, she refrained from laughter, for now.

"Well, I should've known. Have a nice reunion, did we?" He walked briskly towards them. *Oh no,* she thought. *Here we go!*

"Hey you don't know the history behind us, so tread carefully there, buddy!" Rock star already had his defenses up. Not to mention, she could feel the madness and jealousy radiating from him.

"Look you two! Enough already, we are all mature adults. We can talk this out." She tried rationalizing the situation.

"She's here with me, and she'll leave with me!" Romeo was showing a very evil side. She didn't think he had it in him. "Besides, you lost your chance, buddy! When you were all coked out! You fucked things up yourself! So, take your filthy hands of my girlfriend, before I do it for you!"

"I told you to stay away from her! She was off limits to you! I know what you're all about. You don't deserve her, and if she knew what you were all about, she wouldn't have even walked in front of you tonight! So no, I won't take my hands off her. She's mine, always was and always will be!" He stood his ground.

"Hey, I am here, you know. And let me tell you both that no one owns me! So you can both shut up right now!" Her voice went unheard.

"You think because you went to rehab and called her crying your heart out and apologizing that she would take you back? That's why I deleted your messages before she even heard them. She doesn't need your type in her life!" He was so angry he forgot about discretion and let out his secrets. "I had her pegged from the first night I met both of you! And I know your type, which meant it wouldn't be long before she was with me. And here she is, Mr. Rock Star, with me!"

"Well, by the looks of things, that's my cum running down her leg right now. So, it looks like she's with me now!" She stood beside him, shocked. All these things she was hearing. Were they true? And if they were, she didn't know either one of them at all. She was speechless. She just stood there and listened to them argue.

That last comment was the breaking point, which she knew, was near.

Romeo dove at him full out. They both tumbled to the ground, rolling around in the leaves and dirt. They were throwing punches at each other, and she watched the blood spill through the air. She just stood there and watched them beat the shit out of each other. Let them fight, she didn't care. They both deserved what they got. It was dark in the garden, with only a small amount of light spilling over the wall, but she could still see the bruises and bumps forming on their faces. After several minutes of intense fighting, they gave up. They sat on the ground staring up at her.

"Finished? Now both of you can fuck off! I am no one's property. And did you honestly think I wouldn't find out that you tampered with my shit? You don't deserve me. I don't care how much money you have. I never did. And to think you were planning to get me this whole time! So it was no quaint coincidence in the airport? You knew the whole time what had happened? And what, just swooped in like some fucking vulture! You are sick. You have some real fucking issues, you know that! I'm done. Done. Done. Done!" Her voice remained somewhat calm, but her blood was boiling under her skin. And she felt herself on the verge of tears—tears of anger, rage, and betrayal. She turned and walked out of the garden and out of both of their lives and left them both sitting on their asses in the garden of evil.

She hurried back to the hotel room to collect her things. She wanted to be out before he returned. She had no idea where she was going to go, but she knew she didn't want to stay here. The thought of him made her sick to her stomach. He planned the whole thing. He tried to keep her away from the rock star. That was a decision only she could make. He had no right deleting those messages. Thinking back, she did find it weird that he never tried to contact her. She packed her things frantically, throwing everything in her suitcase, not taking the time to fold anything. Pushing it all in so she'd be able to close it, she picked up the dress from the evening, thought about it leaving it, and then thought, to hell with him, she was taking it with her! She was in her jeans and tee shirt again. She was herself again. She wasn't meant to be some uppity girl, surrounded by money and planes and private parties. She lit a smoke from the pack she had just purchased from the cigar shop in the hotel. She hadn't smoked in months. That was another thing she gave up. She inhaled deeply, and as she exhaled, she exhaled the past six months. She was back, just the girl from Canada that drank beer and smoked. That was all she wanted to be. She swung her bag over her shoulder and pulled her suitcase behind her, and threw the cigarette into the half-filled champagne glass on the dresser. She walked out the door of this fake life and back to her own.

Standing out front of the hotel, bags in hand, she had no idea where she was going. But she had never felt more like herself than she did right now.

She lit another cigarette and sat on her suitcase. God, if this wasn't a cliché rock song, what was? She laughed out loud with that thought. The doorman looked at her and smiled. "You need a car, Miss?" he offered.

"No I don't. Thanks anyway." She just sat there smoking her cigarette thinking she'd had enough of private cars and limo drivers. She might just take the damn bus! *Okay*, she thought, *now that's pushing it.*

A car pulled up, not a black rented car. Just a regular car, so there were no worries about it being Mr. Money. But she didn't expect it to be the drummer.

"What are you doing here?" she asked.

"Well, we all heard what happened, and he knew with your temper that you wouldn't be staying here anymore, and he was worried about you, so I came to see if I could take you anywhere," he explained.

"Well, if he was that concerned, why the hell didn't he come himself?"

"Well, he didn't know if you wanted to see him or not, and the way he looks, he couldn't handle another punch being thrown at him, I guess!" She laughed at that.

"Grab the fucking bags! You got beer?" she asked as she jumped in the front seat of the car.

"Yeah, but it's American." He sounded disappointed. She was too.

"Time to go home, my friend. Even the beer is better in Canada!" They both laughed at that.

"Damn straight it is! Yeah, I wanna go home too," he answered.

Rock 'N' Roll Confessions #22

She walked into his hotel room, where the band was having a few beers, and he was laying on the couch holding his beer on his stomach.

"You look like shit, Rocky!" She stood over him trying to sound unconcerned for his well-being even though the sight of his blackened eyes and cut-up face tore at her heart. He did get those war wounds for her, after all.

"So that's the thanks I get for defending your maidenism?" He went to get up and fell back down.

"Maidenism? That's not even a word. And if I recall, you took that right before the fight!" The band laughed at that.

"It's nice to see you guys together again," the drummer said.

"Oh, don't get all sentimental on us here boys!" she said back. Although, it was nice to see them all here together, like in the beginning.

"I thought you guys would be celebrating all night. Congratulations, by the way; well deserved." She raised his beer in salute to them. "Can't I get one of my own?" Someone tossed her a can.

"Cheers!" she cracked open the can and drank it down.

"So, now what?" she asked the group even though it was meant for him.

"We go home!" Salutes and cheers followed from every one of them.

"About fucking time! This place is mental! I gotta go home, where the homeless give you a pencil for your money!" The drummer laughed.

"Yeah and the girls aren't plastic!" Another said.

"And crazy people yell at themselves walking down the street!" They were all in hysterics now.

"Where the beer is strong and the weed is even stronger!"

"And girls are girls." They all stopped and stared at the lead singer.

"What?" In unison they laughed.

"Oh, my boys, let's go home!" She raised her beer again. "But first, let's get pissed!" She laughed wholeheartedly for the first time in years. He stared at her. God he missed her, and them, for what they used to be, instead of what they had all become.

Hours later, he fell into bed beside her, drunk and giggling. His face didn't hurt as much anymore. The alcohol took care of that.

"Does it hurt much?" she asked

"No, not right now it doesn't."

"Damn, it should! What were you thinking?" she asked.

"I never liked that guy. I warned you about him before. I meant it. He's messed up," he explained. "And when I saw you there with him, I knew that was why you had never called me back. I went through some rough shit. Eventually, the guys had enough. We almost broke up, and I knew I had to do something. My girl was gone, and the band was on its way out. Something was definitely wrong. And it was me. So I had to fix it. It's good you weren't around for it, though. It got worse before it got better. And when I realized the way I treated you the last time I saw you, well, actually when I sobered up, the band told me how badly I treated you." She just listened in the dark hours of the morning.

"I felt like the biggest bag of shit. So I tried calling you, and I left you several messages, and I never heard back from you, so I thought, well, it's really done this time, and I deserved it. So I gave up. I wanted you to move on with your life, you know, fuck. It killed me. I never needed you more in my life, and I couldn't do anything about it. You weren't here." He stopped explaining and lay there quiet in the dark. She could feel his tears without seeing them.

Without a word, she slid closer to him, lifting his tee shirt off. She undid his pants and pulled them off. She stood at the foot of the bed and began to undress herself. She was slowly exposing herself to him, and more than just her body; she was exposing her feelings to him as well. He watched as his eyes adjusted to the darkness, and he could see her silhouette taking form. Her breast was glowing in the dark, and the lines of her tender body shaded in the night. He didn't speak another word, and neither did she.

She crawled over his body, kissing his legs, calves, hips, straddling him once she reached the hips. She took his member in her hand and gently massaged up and down. Their eyes locked. She bit her lower lip, holding in her teeth as her hand slid up and down. She bent forward and took it into her mouth. Circling her tongue around in slow motion, all the way down to the base and back up again; rubbing her tongue around the head, her eyes down, her hair falling over her face, brushing the tender skin of his belly. He was breathing harder, his tears still rolling down his cheeks. He tried to hide them from her, but he knew she knew.

She lifted her hips up and onto the shaft, one leg on the floor, one leg bent on the other side of him. Slowly lowering herself on him, she reached down and played with herself. Their eyes locked again. She slid up and down, slow, then quick, then slow again. She rocked back and forth on the head, making him quiver. Never losing eye contact, the muscles in her legs burned. But she didn't want to stop. She was so close, and she knew he was too. She didn't want to lose the moment. She felt his muscles tighten, and he reached up for her waist, pushing her down harder and faster. He moved her body with his arms up and down, up and down. Their eyes still locked, she wanted to look away. It was too intense, but she didn't dare lose contact with him. They came together, and he pulled her forward to lie beside him. They fell asleep in each other's arms, holding onto the moment, for as long as they could.

The Present

Rock 'N' Roll Confessions #23

He stretched his arms way up over his head. He was feeling very well rested, in spite of the past replaying through his head all night. He let his arm fall to her side of the bed, fully intending to wake her up. The bed was empty but still warm, so she wasn't far. He got up and walked to the bathroom, stopping at the door she had left slightly open. Steam was creeping out as he was peeking in. He laughed as he listened to her singing in the shower. It's not that she was a bad singer, it was the fact that she was singing into a shampoo bottle and dancing naked with bubbles in her hair. She looked very cute.

He joined her in the shower and the song. She squealed.

He couldn't keep his hands off her. He wrapped his arms around her slippery body, pushing her out of the water and him into it.

"Hey, I was here first!" She laughed and tried to push her way back into the steamy water.

"Let's share"

"Okay, me first!" She squirted the shampoo at him. He retaliated by throwing a wet wash cloth at her.

"Ouch!" Even though it didn't hurt, she played on it and then threw it back at him.

"Okay, stop, someone's going to get hurt. Stop horsing around. She tried to sound serious and even put on her serious face. It didn't work.

"Oh, look who's all grown up all of a sudden?" He poked and teased her, and she couldn't help but laugh.

Half an hour later they managed to both be showered and dressed. How she didn't know. They carried on in there mostly.

Sitting at his table having breakfast, in one of his button-up shirts, she asked, "So what now?"

"I don't know. Guess we just continue where we left off?" he answered.

"Well, what have you been doing? And why are you still here? I thought you would've been gone off to where the action is."

"No, I gave that up a long time ago. I find it easier to write songs here, at home. Back to my roots." He emphasized the word roots.

"Really? Hmm." She shoved another spoonful of fruity cereal into her mouth.

"For real. I write better at home, and I don't get into any trouble here. I like the quiet life now. I've been writing some different shit, a little more southern rock like, for the next album. What made you come back? Tired of living abroad?"

"Something like that. I got the chance for a permanent position here. Guess I'm tired of living abroad and travelling."

"I could give you a permanent position!" He laughed.

"Oh, I've had too many of your positions within the last twenty-four hours. I think I'm good!" she warned. There was no way she could have sex with him again today. Her body ached from every muscle to every bone.

"I'm not as young as I used to be, you know?"

"Oh tell me about it. I almost had a heart attack last night in the parking lot!" They both laughed together.

"So, can I ask you something?" Hesitation in his voice. He wasn't sure he really wanted to know the answer.

"Ask away!" Another spoonful of cereal in her mouth.

"Why'd you leave, the last time? And why'd you come back? The real reason, because you've been offered that position many times and turned it down." He asked in spite of the answer. He needed to know for his own reasons, and to make sure she didn't do it again. He needed to know she was here to stay. He wouldn't survive her leaving again.

She hesitated before answering, searching her mind for the real reason. She didn't know.

"I don't know. I really don't." He gave her an unsympathetic look. "I mean, we were good. It was just, too good, I guess."

"That's it. You broke my fucking heart because we were too good?"

"No, that's not what I meant."

"So what do you mean? Because that just doesn't cut it for me!" He was trying to keep his voice calm. He didn't want them fighting again. Although, if they followed up with the makeup sex, then …

"I'm fucked up. You know that. I don't like to get too close. I've always been that way. I guess it's more of a leave before you're left kinda thing? We were still really young and stupid. I didn't want to have any regrets."

"So last night, when I caught you at the door, were you going to leave me again? Answer me honestly, because

I can't do it again. You're either here for good or you're not. I need to know."

"I got scared, that's all. I haven't seen you in so long. And then right away, bam! All or nothing. Can't we just go a little slower this time? It's always so intense between us," she answered as honestly as she could. "And is it more than just sex? Not that I'm complaining. I really like the sex. It's good." She stretched out the word good as long as she could.

"Good? It's good? Tread lightly, baby, I'm starting to get a complex!" He smirked with his words.

"It's fucking fabulous! You know that. No one else, and I mean no one else, can take away that hunger. No one else can bring me to my knees every time." She stood up and started walking toward his side of the table, wiggling her hips and her upper body in an exaggerated belly dancing kind of way. She continued in her sultry voice, "Only you make me wild with desire. Only you get so far in, I can't breathe. And only you," she stopped to kiss him. He shoved his chair back to allow her in. She straddled him in the chair, her naked legs aching from last night's adventures, reminding her that she couldn't possibly do it again. Yet, here she was seducing him for more. "Only you, touch my body with such intense emotion." She slid down onto his lap, only to find he had somehow managed to release the snake sometime between fruity cereal and conversation, without her even noticing.

She slid right onto his hardness, and to her surprise, she seemed to be just as ready as him.

"I thought ..." he started to say before his breath was taken away from the feel of her warmth over him. She slid up and down slowly. He felt bruised, as he was sure she was.

He slowly unbuttoned each button of his shirt that she was wearing and caressed the smooth skin of her upper body. His hands whispering over the softness of her skin. He was still amazed at the touch of her skin, so soft. He wrapped his arms around her, pulling her in close to him; she continued to ride him slowly, driving him crazy.

He stood up with her in his arms, and his cock still in her, and cleared the table with one arm. Laying her down on the large wooden structure, he lowered himself onto her.

The sugar spilled over the table, adding to her already sweet taste. He licked the sugar off the side of her leg. He raised himself up and reached for the liquid honey. He held the bottle upside down, letting its sticky thickness reach the opening in the bottle, and he gave a little squeeze and it slid out thickly. Slowly he moved the bottle around to make patterns of sticky honey on her nipples, swirling down her belly, down further to her own sticky sweetness. He threw the empty bottle to the floor and started dragging his tongue over the river of honey on her body. She moaned as she ran her hand over the honey on her tits, and she licked her fingers clean.

"I'm addicted to you," he said out loud, not caring if she heard him. "I can't seem to get enough of you. The way you taste. The way you smell. The way you look." His hands and face were sticky from all the honey; he reached for the fruit bowl and fisted a handful of strawberries, letting the red juice stain her. He rubbed the honey and juice over her body, and then slathered his own chest in the sweet mess. She sat up, her legs still spread wide open, each one on a chair and him standing in the middle. She moved toward him, sliding her hands up his chest through the sticky blend, and she plunged forward to lick his nipples and nipped at them, flicking them with fast movements of the tongue. She reached behind her and took hold of the ice-cold juice jug. She poured a trickle down his chest, making his stomach retract and him gasp for breath.

She slid off the table to her knees, and took in a mouthful of cold juice. With the juice in her mouth, she carefully took him in her mouth as well, quickly before the juice warmed up too much. His cock retracted and quickly grew again in her mouth.

"Holy shit!" He had never felt something so wild before. She looked up at him, her mouth full, and he almost came right there. He picked her back up, turned her around, and bent her over the table where all the remnants of breakfast had spilled. She lay, chest down in stickiness. Her arms straight above her head, her head turned to the side. A few hard thrusts, and he was in the stickiness beside her.

"We can't even have a conversation about sex without having sex. How is it not about sex with us?" She laughed.

"Who cares? If we want to have sex every hour on the hour, fuck it. That's what we do." He laughed back.

"You make me happy. As fucked up as we both are. You are where I wanna be."

"Me too," she simply said.

Rock 'N' Roll Confessions #24

They lounged around his house all day. After the excitement of breakfast, they hung out in the huge bathtub, big enough for four people.

She was lying on the bed, fully naked, as she had given up on trying to keep clothes on around him for now. They touched each other all day, massaging each other and laughing at how sore they both were. She slept in his embrace for the later part of the afternoon.

When they woke up, he continued to search for answers from her.

There was a big hole in their story, and he needed to fill it. She noted his anxiety of her life for the past year or so. Not knowing what she had been up to, why she left, and why she came back and if she would leave again was weighing heavy on his mind. It showed on his face.

"Why'd you leave, babe? We were so good. Fuck, I missed you so much I could feel my heart tearing a little

more every day. I always wondered … well you know."
He looked into her eyes, longing for the answers. His
hand traced her face.

She rolled onto her back and let her mind go back to
a time she tried extremely hard to forget.

The Past

She sat waiting, dressed in tight black leather pants and a new black shiny tank. Her steel spiked heels were tapping on the hardwood floor. He was recording his new album, and she was waiting, something she'd been doing quite a bit of lately. He was already an hour late, and she was getting pissed off with every passing minute. She decided to try him on his cell. A very girlie voice picked up the phone, which surprised her. "Hello?" said the mystery woman's voice.

"Yes, hello. Who is this?" she almost demanded before toning her voice to concern.

"Oh, are you his girlfriend?"

"Yup, that would be me. Where is he?"

"He wanted me to tell you to go out without him. He's still recording and said he'll probably be here all night," the girl informed her.

"With you?" she asked.

"Oh no. I'm done work for the day. I was just on my way out the door when you called."

"Oh, well before you leave, can you tell him, or leave him a note saying thanks? Oh, and underline that three times in red!" She hung up the phone, feeling slightly guilty about slamming the phone on the poor receptionist, if that's who it actually was.

She grabbed her purse and coat and headed out to meet up with her girls at the club.

On her way, she suddenly felt sad. She was disappointed with herself. She was turning into a couple thing with him. Losing herself for him. She hadn't even realized it had happened. Everything was about him, and she seemed to be left waiting on the sidelines a lot lately and was not particularly happy about it. *How did I change without seeing it?* she thought to herself. Never before would she have been waiting at home for him or anyone else, for that matter. She had been in this city for too long, and suddenly she felt the urge to leave and go somewhere, anywhere but here. She clutched at her throat, feeling panic set in. Her eyes were wide open for the first time in a long time. She had lost herself and didn't even know it.

She pulled up to the club to find her girls waiting out front for her. Tonight, she would party with the girls and forget everything else. Tonight, it was all about her.

Staggering through the door, she had intended to go straight home to her own place, but felt that drunken sex craving everyone seems to get at the end of a really good drinking night. She was trying to be quiet as she pulled off her shoes, her feet burning from dancing all night. She slid into the side table and started to giggle.

He had been watching her sneak into the house and laughed at her attempts to be quiet and sober. She hadn't accomplished either of the two. He watched as she swayed from side to side. She hadn't even noticed him standing against the wall.

"Good time?" He laughed as he asked the question.

"Hi, baby!" she slurred. He laughed harder. It was always fun to watch someone else this inebriated. She swayed toward him, trying to be as sexy as possible, and then she ran into the corner of the coffee table.

"Oh shit!" More slurring.

He couldn't help but laugh harder as she fell on the floor holding her knee. She was now laughing at herself. She had the drunk giggles, when everything seemed funny even if it wasn't. He knelt beside her on the floor, the two of them laughing. She tried to lay her head on his chest and ended up knocking him over flat on his back. She laughed hysterically as she tried to tell him something he couldn't make out.

Her hand wandered from his chest downwards, grabbing hold of his package. "Why is he sleeping? Don't you want to fuck?" She tried to be sexy, but blunt was the only thing she could manage at this time. Sexy took too much energy.

"Just like that, eh? No romance? No seduction?" His voice still held a trace of his laughter. There was a smirk to his words. He knew she was just being her drunken self, but still had to raz her a little.

"Oh, no. Not tonight. I just need to get fucked." This was followed by her laughter. She couldn't even say it with a straight face.

She leaned in to kiss him and burst out in laughter right in front of his face. He laughed back at her. "You are too fucked to get fucked." He was enjoying this too much. He couldn't let her just have it; he was being thoroughly entertained by her.

"I." She paused as she stood up. "I am," she adjusted her clothes and held her finger up in a lecturing kind of way, "I am really drunk." The realization of being this intoxicated suddenly hit her. Sex was now the last thing on her mind. She swayed to the side and almost fell over; he jumped up to save her from the fall. Grabbing her arm, he tried to lead her to the bedroom, only to realize she couldn't make it. She was totally wasted. He carried her to the bedroom and laid her on the bed, undressing her so she could at least sleep comfortably. He shook his head. Damn she looked good tonight. If she had only come home two drinks prior, he might have gotten somewhere with her. But like this, he'd be lucky to get it tomorrow night. He laughed at the thought. She hadn't been this drunk in a long time; years, probably.

She was rambling on about something, but he hadn't been paying much attention to it, lost in his own dirty thoughts.

"I'm going away," she muttered.

"Oh you are; where are you going?" he asked and thought, *Now this is going to be good.*

"I'm leaving. I'm going far away. Where I can be me. Not me with you. Me by myself. The me I used to be." He stood there a little shocked. What was she talking about?

Instead of asking more questions, he just listened.

"I'm not me anymore. I'm me with you. Not good. It's not good. I have to go." She tried to get up as if she was about to leave right now, her words not making sense, but at the same time they did.

She had been quiet lately, a little distant. He felt sick to his stomach.

"Baby, you're not going anywhere tonight. You're going to bed."

"Okay. But tomorrow I'm leaving, okay?" She laid her head down on the pillow and fell asleep.

He laid beside her with his arms around her as she nudged closer to him. She wasn't going anywhere, he told himself. She was talking drunken shit. He still didn't get much sleep that night.

She slept most of the day. He paced most of the day, playing around with his guitar. His mind wasn't into it, though. He wanted her to wake up before he had to leave for the recording studio.

He picked up the guitar again and sat in his favorite chair. With his legs spread open and the guitar resting on his leg, he strummed a few notes, frustrated with thoughts of her; he tried to channel them into a song. It wasn't working. He got up and placed the guitar back into the case. He walked into the bedroom and stared at her. His hand ran through his own hair, pushing it off his face. She was hot, even when she was hung over and sleeping with last night's make-up smeared down her face. Her eyes were blackened from her mascara. He couldn't resist the urge to slide in beside her. Her eyes fluttered open. She peeked at him with one eye.

"How are you feeling?" He touched her head softly.

"Not too bad. What time is it?" she asked.

"Late. I have to leave in a couple hours. You slept all day," he informed her.

"Oh shit. I hate when that happens."

"So did you have a good time with the girls last night?" He smiled at the thought of her staggering in last night.

"Hell yeah. Am I enjoying it right now? Not so much." She rolled onto her back and placed her hand on her forehead.

"You were pretty funny last night." He was trying to tread lightly, asking menial questions, even though all he wanted to know was what she was talking about last night with the whole leaving thing.

"I'm sure I was. Did I make an ass out of myself?" She peeked over at him with one eye. *Man, she looks so cute like this,* he thought to himself.

"Not here you didn't; I don't know what you did when you were out with the girls. No one has called yet, so it couldn't have been that bad. Or they're in the same shape you are and are still in bed." He laughed.

"Hmm. Sure, laugh at me, when I'm weak and can't defend myself." She snuggled closer to him. "Come here," she whispered.

You didn't have to ask him twice. He wrapped his arms around her, and his hand headed south right away. He massaged the smooth, wet folds of skin with his fingers, and she moaned.

"Wait ... I have to brush my teeth first." She tried to sit up, but his hands kept her down.

"I don't care." His fingers continued as his mouth joined in. She laid back and decided to enjoy the ride. She felt the stirring in her stomach, the tensing in her legs. He managed to work his way in between her legs, his shoulders keeping her legs open, leaving her very exposed and vulnerable. Her fingers wound their way through his hair, holding his head in place. She felt every lick of his tongue, and spin of his fingers, and wondered why she would ever want to leave this.

Her own hand joined in, dancing circles around her clit while his fingers formed a rhythm of their own. He did play her like an instrument, his favorite instrument, and he couldn't imagine playing any other. He pulled out all stops, giving her multiple reasons not to leave him. She moaned and twisted. She was almost there, and he could feel her muscles tightening up. This is when he wanted to be inside her, when she was so tight from orgasm it squeezed him hard, making it almost impossible to get in. She opened up for him, allowing him to plunge into the tightness; harder and harder he thrust, the friction tearing at his cock. She dug her nails into his shoulders. He held one hand under her ass, giving more power behind him, allowing him to go as deep as possible. Her voice was growing louder with every exaggerated breath; he gave one hard, intense final thrust that brought them both to ecstasy. He collapsed onto her chest, her legs still around his waist. They laid in each other's arms, him hoping this was enough to keep her here, and her wondering if this was enough for her to stay. Neither of them spoke for a while until he whispered, "Stay." His one single word asked her for more than he could express.

"I'll try," she answered, not sure if it was enough.

Rock 'N' Roll Confessions #25

She sat behind the wheel of her car, driving fast before she changed her mind. She was heading east, not really sure of where she was going. She hadn't told anyone she was leaving; she just left. Left behind her comfy apartment, her family, her friends, but most importantly, she left him behind. She left behind the couple she had become with him. She knew deep inside it wasn't fair to him at all, leaving without saying a word. He must've known it was coming. He must've felt the difference in her. She was never one to stay too long in one place. With all these excuses in her mind, she realized she was trying to convince herself that she had done the right thing. She got scared, bottom line. She wasn't ready to settle down, like he was. He was older, had experienced so much more than her. She felt she still had some living to do, and she could only do that alone. She wanted to find her true self before she became someone else. She had seen it, one day.

She was just someone else, not herself, and it scared the shit out of her. She needed to be free—free from him and life as it was.

She rummaged around for her cigarettes, pulled one out, and lit it up. Tears were forming in her eyes. She missed him already, and her heart ached for him. She desperately wished she could have told him and that he would have accepted it. But he would've tried to convince her to stay, and she probably would have, only to feel the same way months down the line.

The radio was loud, the wind blowing in through the window, messing up her hair. She inhaled the smoke from her cigarette and inhaled the scent of freedom. She was doing the right thing. She was on her way to a new life, a new adventure. Excitement ran through the blood in her veins, and the sorrow ran through her heart.

She drove for hours, listening to music, taking in the scenery. The whole way she was remembering the good times she had with him and the bad times. The bad times weighed heavy on her mind, keeping her driving east instead of turning around and heading west, back to him. He was where he wanted to be; he had his music, his recording studio, and his band.

She wanted more for herself and was on the way to finding it—even though she had no idea what she wanted. That was one of her problems; she never knew what she was waiting for. But that's how she always felt, like she was waiting for something. And now she was on her way to figure out just what she'd been waiting for.

She sang along with the radio as she drove her car. Well, actually his car. She had left and taken his car—one of them anyway. At least it wasn't his favorite. It was her favorite. The sudden realization that she had stolen his car just hit her! *Oh my God, he could call the police!* she thought out loud. Why hadn't she thought of this before? She laughed at the thought; she just stole his fucking car! She drove faster in his car, so she had taken something of her life with him, with her. She took his fucking car. She lit another cigarette and kept driving. She turned up the music.

Montreal. She loved this city. She would stop by and surprise her friend. As she pulled into the driveway, she could hear the yelling coming from inside.

Knocking on the door, she came to the realization that no one inside would hear her with all that racket going on in there. So she walked in.

"Hello?" she hollered. Still no answer. Something smashed very loudly against the wall. *Well, this is going to be pleasant,* she thought sarcastically.

A man half-dressed with long, straggly hair stormed past her and slammed the door on his way out. Her friend followed with her next weapon in hand, about to aim at the door when she noticed her. She screamed in excitement.

"What the fuck are you doing here?" She threw her arms around her friend.

"I left." A simple and truthful answer.

"Left? You left the man of your dreams, the sex demon you can't get enough of? You left?" Her friend stared at her with disbelieving eyes.

"Yeah and I stole his car." She stared blankly at her friend before busting into hysterical laughter from saying it out loud to another person.

"Fuck yeah! Where are we going? I gotta get out of this fucking place. Can you believe that asshole that just left was married? He's been crashing at my place for like a fucking month, and the prick is married! Un-fucking believable."

She followed her friend into the house, listening to her ramble. Oh how she had missed her. Something was always going on in this one's life. Her friend grabbed two beers out of the fridge. "Here, you need one of these. So do I."

A case of beer and a bottle of Jack later, they were both in tears from laughter and sorrow.

"What's wrong with me? I mean, fuck he's so right for me, and I keep leaving him. I am definitely broken. I'm fucked right up!" she confided to her friend.

"No, sweetie, you're not fucked. You're young. And dumb." She laughed. "Really, though, you just need to find yourself. I get it. He should too. He'll understand one day."

She drank straight from the bottle and laid back on the couch.

She woke to the sun beaming through the windows. Her head pounding, she looked to see where her friend had crashed last night and could not find a trace of her anywhere. She staggered to the shower.

Just as she was starting to wake up, with the hot water pouring over her body, her friend wiped the shower curtain open. "Hurry up! I'm packed and ready to go!"

"You just scared the shit out of me!" Her friend laughed at her. "And where are we going?"

"Wherever you were going that made you pull up here! That's where we're going! Hurry up!"

"Okay. Okay. I'm hurrying!" That's why she came here. This is exactly what she was missing. Freedom.

"What are you going to do about your place?" she asked as she watched her friend pack up the last of her clothes.

"Fuck it, I'm leaving it. It's not in my name anyway!" She laughed wholeheartedly. "It's in my ex's name!" She continued to laugh.

"Let's go then!" They ran down to the car, throwing their bags in the backseat. Just as they were pulling out of the driveway, the asshole from last night ran up to the car.

"Keep going." She reversed out of the driveway, squealing the tires to a stop, and her friend hollered out the window, "Go home to your wife, fucker!" She flipped him the middle finger, and the two girls drove off without looking back.

They stopped at shitty bars along the way and partied with some pretty questionable characters. She had never had so much fun in her life. She was on a leave of absence from work for a year. She had no worries for a year. One night they picked up a couple guys who couldn't be much older than twenty, if that, and went to a bonfire on the beach with them. They slept in the sand, smoked weed, and got completely pissed. They hung out with those guys for few days in some little hick town. They were partying on the beach every one of those days and nights. Staring up at the stars at night, stoned out of her tree, she would think of him. And then the weed would kick back in, and she would laugh and forget all about him again.

Until one of the guys recognized her. "Okay, man, I've been thinking you remind me of someone, or that I've seen you before or something. And I just figured that shit out! You're that rock star's girlfriend, aren't you?"

"Who me? No, I must just look like her or something." She tried to cover her face. She stood up and began to walk toward the car. It was over. She wanted to move on. She didn't want to be known as his girlfriend. That's why she had left. To become her own person.

"No fucking way! We've been partying with a fucking rock star's girl man! That's fucking awesome!" He high-fived his friend.

"You bone head!" Her friend kicked sand at them. "Fuck sakes, now we gotta go. Assholes!" She rambled on as she tried to keep up with her friend. She turned back around and grabbed the six pack of beer and cursed one more time at them, "Fuckers!"

She tried to find a decent radio station, going through all the channels, not finding much at all. Finally, she hit a rock station, which just happened to be playing one of his songs.

"Great," she said aloud.

Her friend pulled her shades down and let her hair hang in her face, pretending to be one of the guys in the band, and she couldn't help but laugh. They rocked out to his song, sang it really loud, and swung their heads from side to side. They laughed hard and didn't notice the police officer behind them flashing his cherries.

"Oh shit! We're being pulled over!" she told her friend.

"Keep driving! Fuck it!"

"You are seriously fucking crazy! I'm pulling over!"

The officer pulled up behind them and cruised over to the driver's window.

"ID please."

She reached into the glove box and searched for the papers. Stopping suddenly, she looked at her friend, and mouthed, "The car is in his name!"

Her friend gave her the "what?" eyes.

"I stole the fucking car, remember?" she mouthed. Panic was setting in.

The "what?" eyes came again, and then realization.

"Is there a problem, ladies?"

"No, I'm just trying to remember where I put the papers." She tried to stall until she could figure out what she was going to do. Did he report her after all? It had been months and so far, so good.

Her friend jumped in. "Oh my God, you remind me of that cop on that show. You know the one." She gestured to her friend.

"Yeah he does!" She played along.

"No. I don't." He sternly said, but there was a hint of hope in his voice.

"Yes you do! Can I get out of the car? I want to get a better look at you," her friend asked the officer. *What is she up to?* She wondered but didn't care as long as it worked. "Well, technically you shouldn't, but." Her friend hopped out of the car before he finished his sentence. She skipped over to him in her tight, short jean shorts and see-through tank top. She wasn't wearing a bra either.

He was young, probably new to the position. He would fall easily, and she noticed the drool immediately.

Her friend was rubbing her hands up his arms, complimenting him on his hard body; she had turned on the charm. And it seemed to be working. He was checking out her tattoos. She pulled her pants down a little too far to show him one of "her favorites." She had to turn away from them to hide the smile on her face. This was too easy.

"I have the sudden urge to kiss you." She whipped her head around in shock. Was she seriously going to kiss the cop? Oh, she was fucked!

"Well, I ..." Again, she didn't let him finish when she planted her lips on his. She watched through the rear-view mirror as her friend handled his "Billy bat." His hands were all over her, lifting her shirt up, exposing her tits, in the middle of the day on the side of the highway. She watched with a stirring inside herself as her friend bent down and pulled the officers pants down to his knees, taking him in wholly. She was mildly jealous; she hadn't had it in months. Her last time was with him. The ache grew to her heart. She missed him. But her eyes turned to her friend and the police officer. She found her hand sliding into her own shorts, and she took matters into her own hands. She watched as the cop pulled her up and bent her over the trunk of the car and slid in. She felt the rocking motion of the car as he fucked her friend. She felt the intensity as she fondled herself, and she noticed the cop watching her through the window, so she exaggerated every move for him. He knew what she was doing, and he was enjoying it. She challenged him with her eyes; he performed much more aggressively now that she was watching him. Her friend getting all the benefits. She released her tension and let it out with a loud moan, but she continued to watch the two of them on the trunk of the car.

Well, she thought to herself, *this was one way of getting out of a ticket, or jail time.*

When all was said and done, her friend came into the car, sweaty and out of breath, "He still wants to see your papers," she said bluntly and ran a hand through her hair.

"But I got his number. It's all good."

She stared at her friend, thoroughly pissed off, "Are you fucking kidding me?"

"No, he knows the car is stolen. And apparently, your boyfriend wants his car back. I don't know … go figure!" Her friend was trying to fix herself up in the mirror.

She threw her hands up in the air and slammed them down on the steering wheel. This was just fucking great.

"Gotcha!" Her friend laughed hard. "But I did get his number. Seriously, I did."

"You are so fucking dead. I'm so getting you back for that one," she warned her.

"Oh no, honey, you owe me big time for this one! I just fucked our way out of jail, okay? So I think you still owe me!"

She started the car and looked at her friend, "Okay, I can see your point." They laughed as they waved to the officer as they drove away to freedom in his car.

"Oh, and there's a great bar in the next town, live bands. I'm meeting him there tonight." She smiled.

Rock 'N' Roll Confessions #26

They pulled up two bar stools and ordered their drinks. The place was pretty busy. The buzz was that a really good band was supposed to be playing tonight. She did not need any more musicians in her life, so she hoped the dirty cop would be bringing some friends.

He looked different out of uniform, and his friends were just as hot as he was. He made his way over to them, a fierce look in his eyes. When he reached them, he grabbed her friend, picked her right up out of her seat, and kissed her with the same fierceness that was in his eyes.

"Good to see you again, too!" her friend replied with a sexy little smirk.

The band came on, and the drinks just kept coming. She was on the dance floor when a sexy number came on that she loved. She swayed her hips from side to side seductively. She wound down to the floor and back up again, her short skirt revealing the lower curve of her ass to anyone and everyone watching. The dance floor seemed to clear an opening for her little routine, and everyone watched as she seduced the entire audience with her sexy number. Her skin glistened softly from the sweat forming on her; her hair was damp and messy in that sexy kind of way. She ran her hands through her hair and swung her head around slowly as she made slightly sexual movements with her hips and ass. Back down to the floor and up again, the audience hollered in appreciation and encouragement. She had had way too much to drink by this point. Her friend, equally as drunk, came up beside her, joining in on the show. She ran her hands up her legs and stopped when she was face to face with her. She took her face in her hands, tangling her hands into her hair, and she kissed her full on the mouth. The crowd cheered extremely loud. They danced together like lovers, kissing and touching each other in all the right places. When the song was over, the crowd went crazy. She held onto her friend for dear life, laughing and almost falling over.

"Shots!" she yelled to her friend, and as if the cop could read minds, shots appeared. They downed the drinks. "Woo!" They threw their arms up in the air and started jumping around on the dance floor. She had made her way over to one of the cop's friends who had been eyeing her all night. She wrapped her arms around his neck and said, "Hey sailor. Wanna dance?" Her speech was completely slurred, but he could still hear the sexiness behind the liquor.

"Well, I'm not a sailor, I'm an officer of the law. But you're damn right I want to dance with you," he answered with his arms already around her tiny waist, reaching for her ass.

"I always wanted to say that." She laughed. "Okay. So you are an officer of the law." That was really hard to say in her condition. "Do you have handcuffs?" she asked as they danced. His was dick growing with every sway of their dance.

"Yes I do." He looked her in the eyes. She was hot.

"Do you have a gun?"

"Yes."

"Is it big?"

"Yes. Very."

"Is it hard?"

"Find out for yourself." He moved her hand to his big gun.

"Well, well, well, I've been a very bad girl. Are you going to arrest me?"

"Hmm. I think I might have to. I think I might have to cuff you to my bed."

"I don't do beds. Want to go outside?"

"Yes I do." The tall, dark, and handsome cop took her by the hand and led her out to the parking lot.

After today's episode with her friend and the other cop, she had been thinking of her own little fantasy with a cop. They reached his car and started to make out immediately, kissing and grabbing at each other's bodies. He lifted her top up, and she tore his shirt to expose his chest, the buttons popping as she ripped the shirt open. Her mouth kissed the bareness of his chest, her tongue licking the saltiness off his skin. His hands roamed her body, his hands soft on her. "You are so fucking hot." He kissed her madly on the lips.

Then turned her around and threw her on the trunk of his car. "Spread 'em. You're under arrest." She squealed in delight. This was going to be so good. She could feel the ache between her legs. She spread them wide and laid her chest on the trunk of the car. "Am I in trouble, officer?" she asked innocently.

He loved the way this girl played. "Yes you are. You are in a lot of trouble, little lady. I'm going to have to frisk you." His hands moved slowly over every inch of her body, gently squeezing her tits. He slid his hands down her ribs, across her belly, and around to her ass. His hands pushed her short skirt, which was already exposing the crescent shape of her cheeks, up around her waist. Fully exposing her, he slid his fingers into the straps of her panties, and with his two fingers, he wiggled them off her.

She stepped out of them and kicked them to the side. The silver spikes of her heels glowed in the moonlight. She turned to face him, and with a look of mischief, lifted her foot onto the bumper of the car, "You haven't searched me here." Her pussy was fully exposed. He thought he was going to cum right there. This chick was so fucking hot, he couldn't breathe.

He fell to his knees and lifted her in his hands with ease. His adrenalin was raging faster than when he was chasing someone down on foot. His heart beat so fast he thought it would burst. He tasted her sweetness; she held his head in her hands. When she started to squirm, he stood up and thrust himself into her. She held onto his neck and wrapped her legs around his waist, and he fucked her standing up. He held onto the car with one arm to keep himself standing. If he let go, his knees would give out. He was never so fucking turned on in his life. This was so hot. He came quickly, but not before he made sure she did.

Laughing, she said, "We need another drink!" She adjusted her skirt and ran back into the bar, with him moving quickly behind her. He wasn't going to let her out of his sight. He wanted more of her.

She was in the bar when she realized her panties were somewhere in the parking lot. She yelled in her friend's ear, "I lost my panties in the parking lot!" They both laughed in their drunken haze. More shots, more drinks, and more dancing. She didn't know how they were still standing at this point. The cops never left their sides.

Before long, the two girls were dancing on the bar. The cops below them were waiting to catch them if they fell off; it was very possible in their state.

She decided it would be a good idea to jump into the cop's arms; it turned out not to be. She landed on him, and he landed on the floor. Her friend fell off the bar, trying to get down to help her. And they all ended up on the floor. That's when the bartender decided it was time to cut them all off. They left the bar and headed back to one of the cops' houses.

She woke up in the morning sore, tired, and hungover. It was a great night. The phone rang loud and pierced her ears. She held her head. These hangovers were getting to be a bit much. She had on a button-up shirt. *Must be the cop's,* she thought to herself, which made her wonder where her own clothes were. She made it to the kitchen, found water, and was rummaging through the cupboards looking for some sort of painkillers for her head. Mr. Officer of the law walked in. "Good morning, sexy."

"Good morning to you. Is this your house?" she asked.

"Yeah, we share it. Want these?' He held up a bottle and shook the little pills around.

"Hmm. Yes please."

"So, when are you going to return your boyfriend's car?" She almost spit the water onto the floor. He totally took her by surprise. She stared at him blankly, and she couldn't have looked guiltier.

"Sorry?" was the only response she could muster out.

"Well, my friend and I, we're not stupid. Even though, I do have to give you girls credit. That's the best attempt at getting out of jail time I have ever seen. But we still ran your plates." He sat at the table and took a drink from his steaming coffee. *What is it with cops and coffee,* she thought to herself. *What next? Donuts?* She laughed out loud.

"What's so funny?"

"One, I think I'm still drunk. And two, I'm waiting for the donuts to come out!" She laughed uncontrollably. She was still drunk, and her nerves were completely on edge now.

"Oh, funny is it?" He held a smile in his voice. She was so sexy, standing there laughing in his shirt with make-up running down her face from last night. He pulled her so close to him, she fell on his lap.

"You're hot. I'm going to marry you!" He was serious when he spoke.

"No, I don't think so." She thought he was joking, so she joked back.

"Okay, then I'm going to arrest you."

"You're going to arrest me because I won't marry you after knowing you for one night?" She laughed.

"No, I'm going to arrest you for stealing your boyfriend's car." She didn't know how to take his words. Was he just playing around with her?

"I didn't steal it. I borrowed it."

"Well, that's not what he said when we called him."

"Really? What did he say then?" She thought she would call his bluff.

"He said he hadn't seen his girlfriend or his car in months. And he would like them both back."

She felt her heart drop to her knees.

"He wants you to call him." She walked out of the kitchen to look for her friend. She found her wrapped in sheets walking out of a bedroom with the same look on her face.

"He told you, didn't he?" her friend asked.

"What the fuck are we going to do?"

"Send the car back." Her friend was serious for the first time since this little journey begun.

"Fuck." She ran her hand through the front of her hair. "Fuck! I love that car. Now what are we going to drive?" She looked to her friend.

"Hey, it's better than going to jail."

"Obviously." Sarcasm was filling her words.

"Okay, get your shit we gotta go."

Her friend stood at the doorway. "Um, look. I think I want to hang here for a while."

"With the cops? Are you fucking kidding?"

"No, I really like this one. And the sex ... holy shit, the sex is so good!"

"Not now." She dismissed her friend and stomped down the stairs.

"Are you going to call him from here? I have the number if you need it," her bad cop turned good cop asked her.

"I don't need the number. Where are my clothes?"

"Beside me and the phone. You can't leave without calling him, or I do have to arrest you. And as fun as last night was, it'll be a little different this time around." His eyes roamed her body, and he couldn't help but get hard looking at her. He knew she was angry. He could see it in her eyes. He wanted to throw her against the counter and ram himself into her hard.

"I'm not phoning him in front of you. So give me my clothes." She held out her arms, waiting for her clothes to appear in them. When nothing appeared, she stormed out in his shirt. She found her heels at the door and slid them on, slamming the door behind her.

She got in the car and sped off in search of a pay phone.

She stood in the phone booth wearing the cop's shirt and her heels. She didn't even have underwear on; they were somewhere in a parking lot. She held the phone receiver in her hand and dialed the number several times, hanging up before she hit the last digit.

What was she supposed to say to him? She leaned against the glass wall of the phone booth, cradling the phone to her chest. Her heart was pounding, and she felt sick to her stomach.

She dialed the number and let it ring.

"Hello?" A groggy voice answered.

"Hey. It's me." Her voice barely above a whisper.

"Baby, where are you?" He woke up fast at the sound of her voice.

"I'm sending your car back." She tried to be distant, but her heart melted at the sound of his voice.

"I don't want the fucking car! I want you! Do you know I've been worried sick about you! Wondering where you are!" His voice growing louder.

"I'm sorry."

"When are you coming back?" he asked, hopeful.

"I don't know." She kept her answers simple.

"Are you coming back?"

"I don't know." She hung her head down, tears forming in her eyes.

"Fuck, I miss you." She could hear the tears in his voice.

"I miss you too."

"I miss the way you smell. The way you taste. The way you feel." She remained quiet, a lump forming in her throat, and she listened to his words.

"Come home. Be with me. I need to touch you. Don't you want me to touch you? Don't you miss the way I make you feel? The way my hand knows your every spot. They way I fit inside you?" His words were soft and sensual, trying to seduce her back. Her hand glided down her legs, touching herself with the memory of his hand. She imagined him standing there with her in the phone booth. She let a moan, which confirmed she did miss his touch.

"You touching yourself, baby? Don't you wish I was there with you right now?" he asked, envisioning her standing in a phone booth playing with herself; the thought made him hard instantly.

"I want to give it to you right now. I want to slide my cock into you, soft and slow at first, then hard. I want to hear you scream … I want to make you cum."

Her hand was extremely wet. "Yes. I want all of it. I want you. I want you to play with my clit right now, make me cum." She was almost begging him over the phone. He had awoken the hunger in her. Her cum ran down her legs in that phone booth, and she could hear the pounding of his fist on his groin over the phone, could hear the shortness in his breath.

"I'm sorry. I have to go." She hung up the phone, sliding down to the floor of the booth, and cried into her hands. She had to hang up before she got caught up in him again. She needed him soon. Her body ached for him. She hated that she needed him so badly. Her only comfort was that he needed her too.

Rock 'N' Roll Confessions #27

She had stayed in the little town for her friend. As hard as it was, she had adjusted to life in a small town. She did it for her friend. And seeing as how the cops refrained from arresting them, they became good friends.

Her friend asked her to stay for her, her first shot at a normal relationship. Never having much luck in the past, she always ended up with losers—guys with more issues than *Vogue*. So her friend remained with the cop in a very happy and weird relationship. Not weird in a bad way—it just seemed odd to her that her friend would end up with a cop. She was always such a bad girl. And here she was, the bad girl with the good cop. It made sense now that she put it to herself that way. She smiled at the thought.

She walked through the little town. The air had changed from warm summer nights to a brisk coolness, changing the color of the leaves; changing her. It was her second winter here, something she never saw coming. Her own boy in blue was still around; he had fallen in love with her. She used him out of sexual convenience. He was a great guy, but he just didn't do it for her. No one did it for her except him. The hunger was burning inside her stronger every day.

She hugged her sweater in close to her body, attempting to block out the chill. She wanted to move on soon. She could feel the change in herself as much as she could feel the change in the air.

Her friend wouldn't need her much longer. She had found herself and where she was supposed to be. As for herself, she was still waiting. Waiting for what, she didn't know. And at this point, she thought she never would. She knew these thoughts and feelings were about to lead her back to him.

New Year's Eve

She was dressed to kill in a black sequenced dress with black silky thigh highs. She looked at herself in the mirror. Her body suddenly ached, the alcohol driving her mind insane. Her thoughts were only on one thing. She had to go home. She had to find him. Her body and heart couldn't be away from him any longer. She wanted to rip the clothes from her body, she wanted to scream, and she didn't know what she wanted to do first. Her thoughts blurred from the insane hunger that grew stronger by the minute. She was desperate, and she knew her boy in blue was about to propose to her. She had to leave. Right now. She had to get out of this small town where everyone knew everything.

She left the bathroom, grabbed her coat, and wrapped her body in the warmth of the long wool coat. She briefly looked back, took one last look around the bar, and settled her eyes on her lover. She had to leave before he saw her.

She walked out the door into the blowing snow and ran to her car. She left—left all of her belongings, her friend. She would call and explain to her later, knowing she would understand.

She drove through the night, stopping for coffee and gas. She sped down the highway, feeling her stomach drop with the thought of seeing him, touching him. She felt the wetness between her legs, felt the hunger burn. It burned stronger than ever before. She hadn't seen him in so long. She was desperate, desperate for him to touch her on every inch of her body—desperate, for him to take her to that highest level of eroticism. The mental pictures flashed through her head so fast, causing her stomach to drop over and over again, desire burning so deep inside her. The wetness seeped out of her, wetting her legs and the seat beneath her. Panic set in, taking over the hunger for just a moment. Would he still want her? Her eyes teared up at the thought that he might have moved on. Where would he be? Would he take her in his arms, or would he push her away for always leaving him? She drove the entire trip on pure hunger for him. She didn't want to stop to sleep, or eat. Lighting smoke after smoke, her mind traveled to every thought of him; the way he smelled, the way his hair felt in her hands.

The way he held her and tasted her and filled her every opening. Her body ached more, and the hunger grew to insatiable levels. She drove faster.

It was night when she reached home; she went back to her old apartment, which still housed all of her stuff. Her family had kept it up to par. She took a long, hot shower and got dressed in an outfit he wouldn't be able to resist and went on the hunt for him.

She walked into the bar, searching for the darkest, most mysterious stranger …

The Present

Rock 'N' Roll Confessions #28

"So that's it." She looked down, hiding her emotions.

"Baby, I wish you would've just said you needed to find yourself. I didn't realize it was that simple." He took her hand in his, realizing he had lived all his dreams. He had turned them into reality; what he hadn't realized was that they were his dreams. Not hers. She never complained. She let him have everything he wanted, and he took total advantage of it. He suddenly felt like a selfish ass. Why hadn't he seen it before? He looked apologetically in her eyes.

"I'm sorry," He sincerely said.

"For what? I should be the one apologizing. I kept leaving you. I didn't know what I was looking for, yet I dragged you into it every time," she tried to explain.

"You have nothing to apologize for. Believe me. I dragged you along with me through everything, never asking if you wanted to be there or not. And to be honest, I don't think I cared at the time. You were my rock. If you were there, I knew it would be okay. That I would be okay. And that was just fucking selfish. So again, I'm sorry."

"I never saw it that way. Really I didn't. When I wanted to leave I did. It's not like you held me captive." She giggled to lighten the mood. She wasn't good at emotional. It made her uncomfortable. It was one of the reasons she always left. She didn't know how to get close, or didn't want to. As soon as it became too comfortable, she would panic and leave. It was one of her issues.

"Your turn; what did you do while I was gone?" She stretched her naked body across the bed, reaching for his cigarettes. He reached for her ass.

"Oh no! You don't get off that easy. I told you mine. Now you have to tell me your story." She tried to cover her body with the tangled sheets.

He wrestled her onto her back. exposing her body to him again. He couldn't keep his hands off her; he was drowning in the scent of her.

He pinned her hands above her head, and she lay on her back, trying to wriggle free. With his knees, he nudged her legs open. She laughed. "I can't. There is no fucking way I can do it again!"

"Yes you can. Well, I can, so you just lay there and let me." His voice was full of hunger for her. Damn it, he couldn't believe he was about to do it again himself. But just the thought made him grow against her leg.

She gave in and opened up for him, her heart pounding against his chest. He kissed her soft, ran his tongue over her lips. She arched her body toward him. Her hands ran down the tattooed skin of his back, over his shoulders, down his arms. His skin was hot, and she shivered against him. A sudden chill carried its way through her body as she lay next to his heat. His lips travelled from her lips to her neck, licking and tasting the saltiness of her skin. His hands roamed to her breasts, his mouth finding its way there as well. He took her in fully, flicking her nipples with his tight tongue. She held onto his head, her hands tangling in his hair. She moaned and whispered, "Why me?"

"It's always been you," he muffled out in between mouthfuls of her. "Always you." His hands and lips moved down her midriff, flicking the diamond of her belly button ring. He took it between his teeth and tugged at it gently. She spread her legs wider for him and pushed his head down further. Her hand on her forehead, her eyes closed, she enjoyed every flick of his magnificent tongue, every push of his long fingers, every twist. Her legs quivered, her stomach dropped, the heat swelled within her, and she came in his mouth. She rolled on top of him, sliding onto his hardness, rocking back and forth, slow at first. "Only me?" she asked more than stated. She still wasn't sure. But if she was going to stay this time, she wasn't about to share anymore.

"Only you, baby. Only you. Fuck that's awesome. Faster." She gradually slid over his cock, faster and faster. Leaning back, bending him with her slightly, she fucked him as hard and as fast as she could, completely out of breath and energy, she wouldn't stop, wanting to claim her stake in him. "You're mine."

"I know, baby. I know. Fuck me as hard as you can! Make me cum!" he begged her.

She slowed down instead, swayed gently on him, lifting up slightly as she did, and with everything she had left, she pushed him in as far as he could go, as hard as she could, and circled her hips with him inside her as he came. She collapsed on top of his chest. Hot and sweaty, "Now, what's your story?" she asked, exhausted.

The Past

Rock 'N' Roll Confessions #29

He came home to find his house eerily empty. He knew before he looked around that she was gone. He knew she wouldn't be at her own place either; she was gone on one of her soul-seeking journeys. Not knowing when she would be back, his heart sank. He threw his keys onto the side table, grabbed a beer from the fridge, and plunked his ass on the couch. Her scent still lingered in his house. He drank his beer, not knowing what to do with himself other than feel sorry for himself and bask in her scent that would soon be gone. He thought of going to look for her but realized she didn't want to be found. If she wanted him to know where she was, she would have told him or left him a note.

In hindsight, he saw it coming saw the change in her and chose to ignore it, selfishly hoping she would stay with him. The thought made him angry as he emptied bottle after bottle of beer. He lined them up in front of him on the table. The sun had gone down by now, and he found himself sitting in the dark, not wanting to turn any lights on. He was missing her already, and the anger grew inside him. He stood up and cleared the table of its bottles in one hand swipe, sending them smashing against the wall to crash on the floor.

He walked out and slammed the door. Getting into his car, he realized she had left with his other car. Her favorite car of his. Bitch!

Somehow, he swerved his way down the road, finding his way into a local bar. It was just a second-rate bar, tucked into a dark corner of a not so great neighborhood; he walked in and ordered a shot of Jack and a beer. He didn't speak to any one, just drank one after the other until he fell asleep at the table in the corner. It would soon become his favorite hangout.

Night after night, he drank his way through his misery. The band wasn't as busy with the new album complete, so he found he had too much time on his hands. The guys in the band were moving on. One was having a baby with his wife, the other going away for a few months, and the rest were doing their own thing. So he drank. He could've left too, but he waited—waited every day for her to come back.

The bartender became his new best friend in that second-rate bar. He told him stories of life on the road, life with her, and now life without her.

"Buddy, you got to get it together. You come in and get shit-faced every night! Why don't you try looking for her?" the bartender offered.

"Fuck man ... I wouldn't even know where to start," he slurred.

"Well, you ain't gonna find her here! That I know!" He turned to wipe the other side of the counter. It was a slow night, and he was about to sit down with his new friend for a few drinks, even though he knew he didn't need any more.

"I miss her. No! I don't miss her. I hate her! That bitch leaves me every time! Did I tell you that?" The bartender nodded his head; he'd heard this story a thousand times now.

"And you know what? I'm sick of her shit! I don't need her. I don't." His voice went quiet as he realized he needed her more than air at this point. She was his muse. He hadn't written anything in months. He hadn't had sex. Hell, he hadn't even looked at another woman since she left.

The bartender threw his towel over his shoulder and brought two beers to the table. He sat down. "Look for her," he stated and raised the long, brown neck of the bottle to his mouth.

"Where, man, where? Where do you find someone who doesn't want to be found?" He felt lost himself, so if he was lost, how was he to find someone else who was lost?

"She stole your car, didn't she?" the bartender reminded him. Not to get her into trouble, but to get him out of trouble. If this guy didn't find this girl, he was going on a one-way trip downhill.

"Well, she didn't really *steal* my car ..." he started but was cut off.

"No, that's not what I mean. What I'm trying to say is you, can put a call into the cops and if she speeds or whatever ..."

"Yeah, she does speed." He nodded his head, the thought finally sinking in, and smirked at the thought of her speeding down some highway with the cops on her tail.

"The cops will pull her over, and then they'll have to call you. And," he paused and took another swig of the golden liquid and raised his finger, signaling his friend to pause a moment.

"And then, my friend, you'll know where she is." He finished his thought, taking note of the wheels starting to spin his friend's head.

A few nights later, he walked back into his favorite watering hole, carrying his guitar case.

The bartender looked up and saw defeat in his friend's eyes. What he didn't see was the drunken stupor he usually held. He was not quite sober, but not shit-faced like he usually was.

"Well?"

"She's not coming back. I told her to keep the car." He walked to the back of the bar and took a seat in his chair, pulled out his guitar, and stared at it. He wanted desperately to play or write something, but he just stared at it. His heart broken, he had nothing. Music had left him when she did. So he drank.

After a few more weeks of drinking his pain away, puking all over himself, and sleeping in it, he realized he had to do something. After a hot shower, and a good jerk-off session with fantasies of her going down on him, taking him in, and then bending over for him to take her hard, he let himself wake up from the drunken stupor he'd been living in.

He picked up his guitar and started playing again. He wrote song after song. They were different from what he used to write. It was more mature, more southern rock mixed with blues. He poured his hurt into every song.

He was actually starting to like life on his own. He had found himself, his true self, and found music again. He had found real music, not Hollywood shit; his music, his words, real life shit. He was living quite simply lately, and that's what he needed. He needed to keep it simple, keep it real, something he hadn't done in so long, he almost forgot how.

He took his guitar down to the bar and played in the corner for free. Just sat and played his melancholy music for a real crowd and for himself. Night after night, he found himself at the bar, sober, playing his guitar in the corner. No spotlights, no cameras, no screaming fans. He had found himself. And he liked it. He was content with where he was but still wished desperately that she was there with him.

He heard the crisp crack of heels on the hardwood floor but didn't look up. His heartbeat raced inside his chest, and he wanted to look up but kept his eyes on his fingers strumming his guitar.

The sound from those shoes getting louder, heading toward him, and he tried to remain composed. His hands began to sweat. He didn't want to get his hopes up, but he knew it was her before he even looked up. His balls ached, and his stomach turned. He kept playing. His eyes glimpsed the red heels, and he looked up those long, sexy legs wrapped in black stockings, letting his gaze linger on her body for a moment too long until he met her stare. "Hey," was all he could say.

The bartender smirked as he finished wiping the glasses clean. "No wonder he was such a mess," he muttered out loud. And shook his head in disbelief as he watched the vixen ride the rock star she had turned into mush.

The Present

Rock 'N' Roll Confessions' #30

"That's it, baby. Nice, eh? I was a mess without you." He laid his head back on the pillow and stared up at the ceiling.

She had no idea what to say to him. She was expecting stories of women and parties and drugs and good times, not stories of him almost drinking himself to death and wallowing in sorrow the whole time.

"Oh." She had to say something, and that was all that came out of her.

"I had to find my way out of Hollywood thinking. You know what I mean?" he asked, not sure if she would ever understand just exactly what he went through, going from a normal, everyday guy to the mayhem of stardom. And then trying to live a life of normalcy after the hype had settled; sure, he was still famous, but the lights go away for a while when you're not touring. Everything seems to die down, and then you don't know what to do.

"I get it. It was different for me, though. I was with you for a lot of it. And it did get crazy, and I wasn't even famous. I was just there, and all of a sudden I was labeled your girlfriend and was thrown into the papers for everything. Yet I didn't do anything. I felt like my freedom had been stolen. I never wanted to be famous. I needed to find me; me without you, because all of a sudden I wasn't me. I was your girlfriend."

"Fuck if we only talked like this back then. We could've saved a lot of heartache and fights." He stared blankly at the ceiling, finally realizing it wasn't so easy for her either.

"I think we had to go through what we did to get to where we are now. I'm sorry."

"I think you're right, and stop apologizing. You didn't do anything wrong." They laid in silence, wrapped in each other's nakedness, enjoying the scent and warmth of their bodies that seemed to melt into one.

She didn't say anything else. She didn't need to. And neither did he. They both knew this is where they belonged, with each other, and hopefully this is where they would stay.

The End

A very special thank you to all my Facebook Fans, who kept me motivated with their desire to read more, more, more!

Thank you to Albina, my makeup artist and friend who was more excited than I was on picture day!

Special thanks to Ted Samson, my photographer, who listened to me rip apart every picture he took. Well, almost all of them.

A special thank you, to the sounds of rock and roll that filled my late nights; inspiring me along the way.

A final thank you, to my family and friends, for their ongoing encouragement.

This book is dedicated to Julie, Tim, Iggy, Keith, and Matt. Thank you for introducing me to the world of rock 'n' roll.